ALL IT TAKES

LIGHT MY FIRE SERIES

J.H. CROIX

To the families we make in all forms.

Sign up for my newsletter for information on new releases & get a FREE copy of one of my books!

http://jhcroixauthor.com/subscribe/

Follow me!
jhcroix@jhcroix.com
https://amazon.com/author/jhcroix
https://www.bookbub.com/authors/j-h-croix
https://www.facebook.com/jhcroix
https://www.instagram.com/jhcroix/

The woman here to adopt a dog was busy petting a sweet three-legged mutt. Meanwhile, Tiffany Mills stood in the corner of the room, her eyes scanning the bulletin board with photos of cats and dogs and a few of our newest residents awaiting adoption.

I knew Tiffany Mills. She'd been way out of my league in high school. She still was. She glanced over at her friend Alice before her eyes lifted to mine. I felt the shock of her attention and a fiery jolt from her gaze. She crossed over to me, the heels of her cowboy boots striking, almost defiantly, on the tiled floor.

She was wearing a pair of leggings with a silky blue blouse that only brightened her already startlingly blue eyes. A lightweight down jacket topped off her ensemble. She stopped in front of me, peering up as she lifted a hand and brushed back her dark glossy hair.

Fuck me. If I thought Tiffany was beautiful in high school, she was simply stunning now. She had a spray of freckles on her cheeks that I'd never noticed before.

"So," she began as she studied me. "You're running the shelter now?"

I nodded. "Well, it's my mother's baby." My chest pinched a little as I added, "She's recovering from double knee replacements, so I've been helping out."

"Oh, I'm sorry. Will she be okay?" Tiffany asked, her gaze softening.

"I hope she'll be okay. She's convinced she'll be bionic after this, so..." I chuckled.

"Both at the same time?" Tiffany's eyes widened.

I shrugged, my lips twisting slightly. "I'm not so sure it's the best plan. She said since she was resting anyway, it made more sense to do them together."

"It'll be a few months before she can deal with this again." I gestured vaguely around the room and toward the hallway where the kennels were.

"Oh, well that makes sense. But it sounds like she'll be okay?" Tiffany prompted.

"I may have to tie her down so she doesn't get on her feet too early, but yes, she'll be fine."

"When do you start with the hotshot crew?" Tiffany asked. Her eyes flicked to Alice who was still petting the dog. I'd just told her and Alice that I was taking a position on the crew with Tiffany's brother.

"Next week. I take care of the feedings here morning and evening. My mom has tons of volunteers who help out as well, so it won't be too busy when I'm working."

Tiffany cocked her head to the side. I tried to keep my eyes focused on hers, but my attention was drawn downward by motion. Her fingers were sliding back and forth on the hem of her silky blouse and her foot tapped on the tile. I sensed the nervousness emanating from her, and I wanted to tell her not to worry. About what, I had no clue. I forced my eyes up.

"So you'll be on Chase's crew?" she prompted.

"Yup. I just saw him this morning. We worked out together."

She waggled her brows. "Hotshots do have to stay in shape."

My lips tugged into a smile. "We do."

When her lips curled at the corners in return, electricity sizzled through me. Hell, I needed to get my reaction to this woman under control. I was so busy I barely had time to breathe, much less lust after a woman totally out of my league.

When Tiffany smiled, a dimple peeked out at the corner of one cheek. "I don't know what I expected you to be doing now, but it wasn't a firefighter."

I chuckled. "We never know what we'll end up doing. What do you do?"

She blinked before replying, "I'm the new office manager at the vet clinic. I dragged Alice down here to adopt a dog."

I grinned as we looked over at them together. Alice was petting a three-legged dog who'd been dumped here at the shelter. The animal was happily soaking up Alice's generous attention.

When I glanced back at Tiffany, she was biting her bottom lip. Seeing her teeth denting that plush surface sent a fiery sizzle down my spine. I took a quick breath, trying to quell my body's response to her.

Her gaze collided with mine, her thick dark lashes sweeping up. Tiffany had felt unattainable to me in high school. She'd kept her distance thoroughly. Every guy had wanted her, myself included. To my knowledge, she'd never even had a boyfriend back then.

"I haven't seen you around since I came back," I offered.

Uncertainty chased through her eyes as she held

my gaze. Her fingertips were still worrying the hem of her shirt, and that urge to protect flashed inside.

"I just moved back recently," she replied.

Alice called over, "She's the one."

"She's all yours." I tore my attention away from Tiffany.

A short while later, I watched as they walked out with the newly named Honey who was dancing happily on her lead at Alice's side.

Tiffany's hips swung with her easy stride. She looked over her shoulder, catching my eyes from a distance and once again sending a jolt through my system. When I turned away to close the door, I told myself I didn't have time to think about any woman. As if to prove my point, my cell phone vibrated in my pocket with a text coming in.

Chapter Two

TIFFANY

I powered down the computer in the reception area at the veterinarian clinic where I was the office manager. I'd started this job last autumn, not long after moving back to my hometown of Willow Brook, Alaska. Just a few weeks ago, we had started closing early one day a week. It gave Alice, my boss, and the veterinarian here, time to catch up on documentation.

Walking down the hallway, I peered into the break room where she was situated with a sandwich and a fresh cup of coffee from Firehouse Café, a local favorite coffee shop.

She glanced up, her gaze thoughtful. "Should I be paying you more?"

I eyed her curiously. "You already pay me above market rate for my position," I pointed out.

"Is there such a thing as a market rate for an office manager at a vet clinic in a small town in Alaska?"

My brows hitched up, and I shrugged. "Not specifically, but I've worked in human resources before, and you're paying me more than I got at my last job in Seattle. Trust me, I'm good. Why are you asking?"

She took a swallow of coffee before replying, "Because I was just reviewing that checklist you made for me for my daily paperwork and realizing I don't know how I could've done this without you."

Alice Hall had grown up in Willow Brook, just like me. We'd both moved away for college and found ourselves returning to town around the same time. Alice had been offered the opportunity to fully take over this veterinarian clinic after the last owner had developed dementia and was no longer able to run it. While Alice was fully trained to handle all of the veterinarian aspects, she'd immediately searched for someone to help with the business side of things. That someone was me. I loved working here because organizing things was my jam.

I smiled, feeling a flush of pride. "I'm glad to help. It's my job."

"Well, thanks for everything. And don't stay out after dark tonight. There's supposed to be a snowstorm coming in."

"This is Alaska. There's a snowstorm almost every week."

She rolled her eyes. "Be careful anyway."

I stared down at the little boy standing in front of me. The moment my eyes collided with his dark-brown gaze, I felt as if I'd been punched in the chest. The jolt of familiarity was shocking. The little boy, who I'd just met seconds ago, eyed me. His gaze was assessing and curious with a hint of guardedness to it.

The woman waiting beside him cleared her throat. I realized I hadn't said a fucking word since I'd opened the door.

"Hi, I'm Wes," I finally said. "Come on in." I opened the door wider and gestured them through. I breathed a silent sigh of relief that the house was clean. Even though I was a bachelor, I was not a slob.

The woman, whose name had promptly flitted out of my thoughts, placed her palm gently on the little boy's shoulders as they walked in. The potentially tense moment was saved by the overenthusiastic rescue dog I was fostering, who came galloping in from the kitchen. The dog in question, Nilla, spun in a circle around my legs before greeting the visitors with her nose.

As Nilla sniffed up and down the little boy's legs, a smile cracked across the boy's face. When he peered up at me, the hesitance and innocence in his gaze twisted my heart. "Can I pet her?"

I chuckled. "Her name is Nilla. I don't think she's going to let you avoid it."

The boy knelt beside the dog. Nilla was a sweet girl and happily rolled on her back, showing off her belly and licking his palms.

The woman smiled at me, offering, "Sorry this is such short notice."

"It's no problem," I said even though it felt as if a meteor had landed in my life when I got her phone call yesterday.

Eight years ago, I had agreed to be a godparent to this little boy. Honestly, that commitment had slipped my mind. Even though I'd stayed in touch with my best friend from college, George, we'd both moved to different areas so our contact had been limited to our weekly online video game chats. He had been one of the closest friends I'd ever had.

The woman glanced over at Ross, George's son. I'd just learned George had died a few days ago. "I'm thinking perhaps we could talk privately," she said, her tone low.

I nodded. "Do you want to take Nilla for a walk?" I called over to Ross, thinking that would give us a few minutes of privacy.

Ross jumped up quickly. "Can I?"

"Sure thing. She won't run away. In fact, she'll just walk beside you. She's due for a potty break."

We walked back out the door, and I gestured over toward the trees to one side. "That's the poop zone."

Ross burst out laughing. "I like you."

I smiled down at him. "I said it before, but I'm

Wes. It's good to see you." I *had* met him before, but it was back when he was a toddler. I was certain I was all but a stranger to him.

He nodded quickly, a shadow flitting through his gaze. We stared at each other. For a moment, I could've sworn my friend was living inside his son. It was like looking into George's eyes. Ross had the same straight dark brows with a familiar furrow between them.

"Just come back inside in a few minutes."

Nilla stayed at his side as they walked down the stairs. If she could've held his hand, she would've. She was that kind of dog.

After the social worker took a long look and seemed satisfied that Ross was content playing with Nilla, she followed me back into the house. Her name jumped into my recollection: Eileen. I gestured toward the windows, commenting, "We can stay right here to keep an eye on him."

Eileen cast me a quick smile before nodding, her eyes arcing about the space. I'd just finished building this house last year. When I took the job with a hotshot firefighting crew, I'd stayed with my mother for a month or so while working fast to get this place ready. It had been a half-finished house that someone else had sold off because they ran out of money.

I'd lucked out. Whoever had designed it initially planned a square with a courtyard in the middle. The main area had a wide living room with tall ceilings and windows all across the outer wall facing what I eventually intended to be a garden area. To one side was a kitchen that also had a bathroom and laundry off it. The bedrooms were on the other side down a short hallway. There was a main bedroom with a bath as well as two smaller rooms. The last side of the square around the courtyard was a garage. While I didn't mind the snow, it was a relief to have protected parking.

Eileen's eyes made their way back to me. "Nice place," she said.

"Thank you." I took a quick breath. "Now, I guess, fill me in."

"Well, as I mentioned on the phone, you are listed as a godparent. This was completely unexpected, and there's no other family for Ross."

I tried to breathe slowly and ignore the subtle sense of panic building inside. When someone asked you to be a godparent, it seemed like a formality, not something that would ever become a reality.

"What happened?" I asked.

"They were driving home during a rainstorm. A power line had fallen over the road, and they drove over it. Obviously, there's no way to know, but the police assume they didn't see the line on the road since it was dark and rainy. When they drove over the line, it tangled in the undercarriage of the car and brought two electrical poles crashing on it." She threw a hand up in the air, letting it fall. "It's heartbreaking."

"Oh my God," I whispered, almost to myself. "Does Ross know what happened?"

"As far as I understand, someone at the police station explained it to him."

I scrubbed a hand through my hair, feeling befuddled and overwhelmed and instantly thinking that the way I felt must be nothing compared to what Ross was feeling.

"George and Sarah were good parents. They doted on him," I murmured, still in shock. "The last time I talked to George was—" I slipped my phone out of my pocket, tapping to open the screen and scrolling through my texts. "We play an online video game together usually once or twice a week and chat then. We texted two weeks ago and had a phone call the next day. I just texted him the other day, wondering why he hadn't been online to play. We were really close friends in college and worked together for a little while afterward. He and Sarah moved, and then I moved, and you know how it goes. But I saw pictures of Ross."

I looked out into the yard. Ross was throwing a stick for Nilla, who was happily fetching it.

Eileen nodded when I brought my attention back to her. "There is no family listed to contact. They actually had a will. Honestly, at their age, that's kind of a surprise. They weren't that old."

My lips twisted. "Nope, they weren't. George was thirty-two, like me. Sarah was a lawyer. She thought things through like that, so I'm sure she made sure they had a will." I paused and looked out at Ross again. "Obviously, this is a shock for me, but I'll take him, and we'll figure it out."

"Well, there's one other thing," Eileen said.

"What's that?"

"There's another godparent listed. The will requests that you share guardianship."

I whipped my gaze back to her. "Oh? Who is that?"

"Huh?" That was all I could manage.

I had taken this call on speakerphone because I was busy updating the benefits in the new payroll system I had set up for Alice. We'd tested a few out and settled on a favorite. Honestly, it was my pick, and Alice was game-enough to go along with my preferences. It was genuinely the easiest one to deal with, so if I wasn't here, Alice could stumble her way through it.

I stared down at my phone screen, part of my brain wondering if this was some kind of joke.

"You're listed in the will as one of the godparents," the woman said.

"Sarah's dead?" My voice had a hint of panic in it.

Sarah was one of my best friends from college. She'd lived in Seattle near me for a few years after college with her husband before they moved to a smaller town in the foothills of the Cascade Mountains. Their life was happy and together. She was a lawyer, and they had a little boy. My brain spewed out this list of facts as if it would confirm Sarah was definitely not dead.

"Yes, she and George died in an accident. I'm sorry to shock you."

"Where is their son?" I blurted out.

"Ross is currently with the other person listed as a guardian in their will. There are two of you."

"Oh," I murmured. "Sarah mentioned that George asked one of his close friends. You know when someone asks you to do this, you don't really think about it. I mean, you do, but you don't ever expect anything to go wrong." My voice was strained.

Alice appeared in the doorway behind the desk, clearly hearing my tone from down the hallway. The vet clinic was closed for the afternoon, so we could get caught up on paperwork and things.

She cocked her head to the side, mouthing, "Are you okay?"

I shook my head, gesturing for her to sit down in the other chair behind the desk.

"I do understand that. I'm sure this is a lot to take in," the woman said slowly. "I'm in town this afternoon because I've just met with the other godparent. He said Ross can stay with him for now, but I'd like to talk with you. Both of you are listed in the will, so we should discuss planning."

"Oh my God, oh my God," I repeated. "The other godparent is in Willow Brook?"

"Yes, that is the case. Sarah was from there, correct?"

"Uh, sort of. Her parents lived here for a few years in high school, but they moved away."

"Ah, I see. I guess that's how her husband met one of his best friends. Is it possible for me to meet with you this afternoon? I drove here from Anchorage."

"Uh, sure," I said slowly, trying to pull my thoughts out of this weird rut where they'd fallen.

I was dealing with the shock of learning one of my closest friends had died, and now, apparently, I might be responsible for raising her son. Oh my God.

"Okay, can you let me know where to meet you?"

"I work at Willow Brook Veterinary Clinic. It's right off Main Street on a side street." I quickly recited the address. "We're actually closed to patients for the last hour today, so it's a good time for you to stop by. You can park in the back and knock on the back entrance."

"Okay, I should be there in about fifteen minutes. Thank you."

I heard the line click, and I tapped my phone screen to make sure the call had ended. I swiveled in my chair, my mouth hanging open as I stared at Alice. "Sarah Ralston died. Do you remember her?"

Alice scrunched her nose. "Didn't she live here in high school?"

"Yeah. She was my best friend. We ended up at college together in Seattle. She and her husband died, and I don't even know how. I agreed to be their son's godparent, but I never thought anything would happen to her!" I burst into tears.

Alice reached out, clasping my hands with hers where they rested limply on my knees. "Breathe." She released one of my hands and snatched a tissue out of the box on my desk, handing it to me.

I sucked in a deep breath before blowing my nose and dabbing at my eyes. "That woman"—I gestured to my phone—"says she's a social worker. I guess she works with the court in cases like this and was assigned to help facilitate making sure their son is cared for. She's coming here to talk to me and said there's another godparent. What do I do?"

Alice squeezed my hand before releasing it. "Do you want some tea or coffee?"

I took a shaky breath. "Coffee. I needed some anyway."

"Come on. Let's go in the back while we wait."

I blindly followed Alice to the break room, watching as she quickly made a pot of coffee. It was ready in a few minutes. I sat at the table, feeling numb. She sat down across from me, handing me a mug.

"Here's the thing. It sounds like he's already staying with someone, and you just need a little time to adjust to this. I'm sorry about Sarah."

I shook my head. My chest ached. "I'm still trying to absorb the information." I took a gulp of coffee, the bitter flavor a jolt to my system. "Holy shit. I don't know what to think. Are you anyone's godparent?" I asked, feeling as if I'd been tossed in the ocean without a life raft. I had no idea what to do.

Alice shook her head. "No one's asked me. For what it's worth, most people don't think something will happen to people they love."

"I'm not going to run away from my commitment."

"Just breathe," Alice repeated.

There was a knock on the back door, and Alice leaped to her feet. "I'll let her in." She paused just as she began to turn out of the doorway. "Do you want to meet with her privately? Or would you like me there?"

"If you don't mind, it would help to have you here. I'll probably forget half of what she tells me."

Alice nodded quickly and hurried down the hallway. A few minutes later, the three of us were sitting at the table in the break room. The social worker, Eileen, had accepted a cup of tea. She had already summarized what happened. Sarah and George had died from when they drove over a downed power line and it brought two electrical poles down on their car, crushing them instantly. I was still stunned and my heart hurt, as if someone had knocked it hard and cracks were spreading.

"Oh my God," I repeated.

Eileen was politely nodding. "Ross is all set for the weekend. I've already arranged a meeting with the executor of the will. I'm just the messenger. Whenever something like this happens and there isn't any family listed, they call the state. In this case, there is a will in place and a law firm in Seattle handling it. They connected with a local attorney here since both of you are here."

"Who is the other godparent?" I finally thought to ask.

"Wes Stuart."

"Wes? From the animal shelter?" I prompted.

"We do all the vet care for the shelter," Alice chimed in.

"That's the one," Eileen replied with a nod. "His mother runs the shelter, and he helps out. He's also a firefighter. Ross is with him for now. I had a little more trouble getting your number. The one in the paper-work was out of service."

"That was probably my old cell number in Seattle. I wanted to have an Alaska area code, so I changed it after I moved," I said, still trying to get my brain to absorb this flood of information. "I just changed it a couple of months ago."

Eileen shrugged. "I found you. So you know Wes? He mentioned he knew you."

I nodded. "We don't know each other well. It's a small town, but I was with Alice when..."

I was so grateful Alice was here. She jumped right in to fill in the blanks of every sentence that I couldn't finish. "I was looking for a dog to adopt, and Tiffany came with me."

"You knew each other in high school too?" Eileen prompted.

"Yeah, but we weren't close. We were a few years apart, and you know how that goes. A few years feels like nothing now, but in high school, it feels like forever."

Eileen nodded. "I'd suggest you take some time to think about how you're feeling. The will lists both of you as guardians. You don't have to accept it, but..." She handed me a sheaf of paperwork. "They specifically stated they want both of you to care for him in the event they are not able. They clearly trusted both of you to be reasonable and to be able to work together in the best interests of Ross. Given Wes's job situation, it might be helpful for both of you to be involved."

I felt like I was trying to slog through quicksand to get my thoughts to catch up to the situation. "What do you mean?"

Alice's gaze slid to mine. "He's a hotshot firefighter. They're gone a lot in the summer." She shifted her focus to Eileen. "My husband, Jonah, is also a hotshot firefighter."

"Oh, oh! Of course. I'm sure we can figure this out," I managed.

Somehow, we continued talking while my thoughts spun. A while later, Eileen left her business card with me, assuring me she'd see me Friday at a meeting with the local attorney and the attorney from Seattle via videoconference.

After Eileen left, I stared at Alice.

"Holy shit."

Chapter Five

TIFFANY

The evening before the meeting, I wondered if I should try to get ahold of Wes. I was a bundle of nerves. My grief was starting to break through the shock of the news about Sarah's death.

The following morning, I made myself dress nice. It wasn't like I was a slob at work these days, but at the vet clinic, you had to be somewhat practical. As the receptionist, I didn't handle the pets the way Alice did, but at any moment, I could be called upon to wrangle a loose dog, or parrot, or goat, as was the case just last week.

I pulled out my city clothes this morning, wearing a fitted silk blouse that flared around my waist with a navy pencil skirt that had a little ruffle at the bottom and low heels. I smoothed my hands over the skirt as I studied myself in the mirror. Maybe this was ridiculous, but I didn't want to look like a slouch at the meeting with the attorney.

After a call to my father, he had put me in touch with his friend's daughter who was one of only three lawyers in Willow Brook. She had assured me she would review the paperwork and be available for any questions and explained she was the local attorney coordinating with the firm in Seattle.

A short while later, I was walking down a hallway off the side of the reception area at the attorney's office. I was glad I knew I was going to see Wes so I could brace myself. When I walked into the conference room, Wes was already seated at the table, and his eyes lifted to mine. It felt as if a flame flickered to life, racing across the space between us when our eyes met.

Wes stood from the table. Even though we already knew each other, I inexplicably approached him and thrust out my hand. "Hi!" I squeaked. My tone sounded too bright, almost harsh to my own ears.

My pulse kicked off at a fast gallop when his fingers curled around mine. I tried to take a deep breath to slow my body, but my lungs weren't having it. All I could do was pull in a shallow breath of air. I did *not* squeak around anyone, much less men. I was deeply cynical about men and had mastered the art of being dismissive. I wasn't even faking it. I truly did not give a shit about men and wanted nothing to do with them. Except that not giving a shit wasn't working too well in the presence of Wes.

Wes's brows arched up, and his cognac eyes studied me. "Hi, Tiffany."

"Hi," I repeated.

Another voice chimed in, "Nice to see you, Tiffany." Turning, I belatedly noticed Eileen waiting.

"Nice to see you," Wes offered as I released his hand after holding it for way too long.

"Uh, you too." Again, with the squeaking. Ugh.

Eileen stood from the table, smiling at us as she gestured to a woman beside her. "This is Tasha Keller. She's the attorney handling the guardianship locally."

I looked over at the woman, and I could've sworn I recognized her. She pushed her glasses up on her nose as she stood from the table. "Hi, I'm Tasha."

We all sat down, and I said, "I swear I recognize you, but I can't quite place you."

She shrugged. "I was in high school with both of you. But two years behind, so you probably don't remember me."

"Wait a second!" I exclaimed. "Your mom was Mrs. Keller, the attorney who did that fun presentation on being a lawyer in high school. I loved that! Even though I didn't end up being an attorney," I hastily added.

Tasha smiled warmly. "That's her."

"So you're a lawyer, then," I stated the obvious.

"I am. This is actually my parents' practice. I slipped right in."

I glanced around the room. "Where's Ross?" Beyond the emotional shock of my friend's death, I'd been anxious about meeting the little boy who I was now partially responsible for. The anxiety was big.

"He's with my mom," Wes explained. "I checked with Eileen, and she didn't think it was the kind of meeting he needed to be present for."

I nodded. "That makes sense. How is he?"

Wes lifted one shoulder in a shrug. "Okay. I guess. But probably not. His parents died last week. I'm still in shock at the news, and I'm sure he is. Fortunately, he loves the dog I'm fostering. They've watched a lot of TV together."

I pressed a palm to my chest, my heart aching at

the thought of Sarah's son. "It's so sad. I'm still in shock. Did you know Ross?"

One of Wes's brows hitched up. "I do now. If you're asking if I spent much time with him before, no. Honestly, the last time I saw him, he was maybe three. I stopped by for a visit. After they moved out of Seattle, I just didn't see them much. What about you?"

"I saw Ross before they moved away from Seattle. He was maybe two? I knew Sarah obviously. We were friends in high school, and then we went to college together. We stayed in touch, but I can't imagine Ross would remember me."

Eileen interjected, "This is startling for everyone. Fortunately, the will is structured as such that you both have guardianship should you accept it."

I looked at Wes, he looked at me, and then we both looked at Eileen together. I was a bundle of nerves and more unsettled than I should've been because, for God's sake, Wes was distractingly handsome.

I sucked in a quick breath. "So what do we do?" I addressed my question generally to everyone as I looked around the table.

"What would you like to do?" Tasha asked, her tone gentle.

I reflexively looked toward Wes, experiencing a jolt when our eyes met. We both shrugged.

"Look, we can do this. They obviously wanted us both to be a part of his life," I said.

Tasha chimed in, "With Sarah being an attorney herself, the will is clear. You can back out, but there is no backup family. Both of Sarah's parents passed away in the last few years. George stated he had limited contact with his family and did not want them involved."

Wes piped up, "Definitely not. He was not close to his parents. I don't have all the details, but I know that. Do we need to worry about them trying to do anything?"

Tasha shook her head. "Fortunately, they made it very clear in the will by specifically stating that they did not want his parents to have any say. They have a trust set up for Ross. There is no financial benefit to either of you, and all money is directed toward taking care of him. Honestly, Sarah did most of my work for me, but I'm here to explain and offer feedback if one or both of you chooses not to do this."

Even though I felt as if my life had careened off the tracks, my heart knew the answer. "Ross can stay with me full-time or part-time or whatever." I looked over at Wes. "I know how your job schedule is. Maybe we should work out some sort of arrangement where we alternate?"

Chapter Six

WES

Tiffany's big blue eyes held mine as I tried to ignore the fiery sizzle of heat running through my system. I forced my attention to the matter at hand.

"Obviously, I'm all in. I'm glad you realize what my job is like, but would it be better for him to be in one place? I'll be honest, my parents broke up, and bouncing back and forth between them was not great for me."

Tiffany cocked her head to the side and pushed her glasses up on her nose. This was the first time I'd seen her in glasses, and she was way too sexy. She was already beautiful, but now she gave off this hot librarian vibe. In fact, I wanted to take her to a library and do all kinds of things with her. Except this was a serious meeting. We were talking about the welfare of a little boy for whom I was responsible.

She took a quick breath before nodding. "I understand."

"You do?"

"Look, we don't need to get into all the details, but I had one very stable parent and one not-so-stable parent. I was forever grateful for my father, but it wasn't so much where I stayed but that I knew what to expect."

"Ah, I see. We'll find a way to make it work. With my schedule during fire season, he'll need to be with you then."

Tasha glanced back and forth between us, her eyes a little wide. "This is ideal. Honestly, I work with parents who can't agree on anything for their own children."

Tiffany shrugged. "Maybe it's because we don't have any baggage between us. Obviously, we both want to keep our commitment. I'm sure neither one of us thought it would come to anything when we said we'd be a godparent, but it has. So here we are."

When Tiffany's eyes caught mine and our gazes locked, I felt something shift inside me. As if a door that had been locked and bolted shut was abruptly kicked open. I forced myself to focus, replying, "That about sums it up. So..." I glanced toward Eileen. "Does Ross know the situation?"

"Since we weren't sure what the decision would be, all he knows is that he's coming here because both of you were friends of his parents," she said.

"Has he said anything about his parents?" Tiffany asked, her tone soft.

"I told him I was sorry," I explained. "All he said was he was too. I'm not sure he's really absorbed what's happened."

Tiffany nodded. "I get it intellectually, but I'm still in shock that Sarah is gone. I keep thinking she'll text me, and I'll realize it was a mistake."

"Do we need to sign anything?" I asked.

Tasha nodded. "You do. I have all the paperwork drawn up. Something to consider in the long run is adoption. You can remain his guardians, but that's an option."

"How is that different?" Tiffany prompted.

"Guardianship can be contested at a later date. Adoption can't," Tasha replied.

"Who would contest it?" I heard myself asking.

Tasha shrugged. "You just never know. I don't recommend making a decision about adoption today. I'm just letting you know the option is there for the future."

Tiffany and I glanced at each other and then back at Tasha with Tiffany replying, "Okay."

A short fifteen minutes later, we were walking out together with our official guardianship paperwork in hand in two separate manila envelopes. Eileen was going to go with us to introduce Tiffany to Ross. The plan was for him to stay with me for the weekend while Tiffany got a room ready for him at her place.

Tiffany stopped beside my car, tapping the key fob in her hand. "Your car?" I nudged my chin in the direction of the car beside my SUV.

She nodded. "I'll follow you?"

"Sounds like a plan."

Those big brown eyes blinked up at me. Ross had his hand buried in Nilla's thick white fur. He was holding that sweet dog like she was a life boat in choppy water. I suppose she was. Eileen had just left.

"This is a lot to take in," I offered softly.

Ross blinked, looking down at Nilla. "Can Nilla come with me when I stay with you?"

I looked over at Wes. This was another question in the long line of inquiries that I felt as if I'd been pummeled by since the phone call yesterday evening.

Wes nodded, mouthing, "As long as it's okay with you."

"Of course," I said quickly, relieved that Ross was focused on Nilla and not me and Wes.

Ross's eyes lifted again, and I saw the sheen of tears there. I didn't know how it was possible that I could be so fiercely protective of this little boy inside of only half an hour, but I was. I wanted to take care of him, to keep him safe, and to make sure nothing bad ever happened again in his life. I loved dogs, and

Alice had been joking with me that I had to adopt one soon. I just hoped I wasn't stealing Wes's dog.

Wes was sitting beside me on the couch. His elbows were resting on his knees with his hands laced loosely together. I was beyond relieved he was here. We'd been thrown into this together.

"You can count on us," he was saying to Ross. "We know this may feel strange and big and probably more than you ever expected to deal with, but we're here for you."

Ross looked over at Wes, asking, "Can I play video games there too?"

I deduced they'd played some video games.

Wes's voice was gruff when he replied, "Absolutely. I promise. Tiffany's fun too. She might even know how to play video games."

"Actually, I do," I offered quickly. "I have an older brother who works with Wes. He taught me how to play video games. I might not be as good as Wes, but I can hold my own."

I made a mental note to check with Wes about what kind of game console to get. I did know how to play a few, but I wasn't a serious gamer by any stretch.

Ross looked between us, nodding solemnly. "Where will I stay tonight?"

"You're with me for the weekend. Tiffany is going to get a room all set up for you. I need to work on that too."

"You already got a bedroom ready for me," Ross said.

Wes shrugged. "I let you stay in mine. I'll get the spare room here furnished so it's all yours."

My heart felt like it might crack when Ross wrapped his arms around my waist before I left, squeezing me tight for a moment. I smoothed my hand over his hair and realized this little boy probably felt so lost.

Wes followed me out to my car, stopping beside the door. He rested his hand on the top of the door after I had opened it. My pulse felt as if someone had spurred it in the flanks, urging it forward faster and faster. I took the moment to study Wes. This man was *all* that and then some with his rumpled dark-honeyed hair and espresso eyes. Also, nature had been ridiculously generous with his mouth. His face was all hard sculpted features, his nose a little prominent, and his cheekbones strong as they angled down. His lips were warm and inviting. My eyes dropped down, tracing along the lines of his broad muscled shoulders and the way they filled out his shirt.

Wes cleared his throat, and my eyes whipped up. "Sorry, just zoning out," I murmured, my voice coming out raspy. It wasn't exactly a lie. I *was* zoning out. I was completely overwhelmed with my life suddenly involving shared parenting duties with a man I didn't know all that well. I was still trying to absorb the fact that one of my closest friends had died.

"There's a lot going on," I pointed out.

Wes pressed his tongue on the side of his cheek as he nodded, his lips kicking up in a wry smile. As if prompted, my belly did a quick flip, one with a flourish.

"That's one way to put it. So Nilla is a rescue I was fostering because we didn't have room at the shelter. I hope you don't mind that we're adopting her. Conveniently, since my mom runs the shelter, she already formalized the paperwork for me," he offered.

"Of course I don't mind. I work at a vet clinic. I

love animals. She'll be Ross's dog and she can just go with him wherever he is. That'll be okay, right?"

"I think it'll probably help him. Maybe we could plan to get together this weekend and take him pet shopping. We could get dog beds and all the things to have at both of our places," Wes suggested.

I felt my lips stretching into a smile. "You're a smart man, Wes Stuart."

He smiled back at me, and butterflies took flight in my belly, sending a scatter of sparks through me.

"I try. This whole thing is kind of... unexpected."

"No shit," I said flatly. "Look, I'm guessing we have a lot to talk about that maybe shouldn't happen in front of Ross. We'll have to talk about school and more."

Wes's eyes widened. "I didn't even think about school."

I nodded vigorously. "We need to enroll him, like yesterday. Eileen mentioned it's best to get him started on a normal schedule as soon as we can. I'll call the school on Monday. Let's plan to go talk to them together."

"Whatever you think."

"It doesn't have to be whatever I think."

"I know, but I'm trying to be agreeable here."

I took a quick breath, closing my eyes before opening them as I let it out slowly. "I know. You're going to get to know me *real* quick, Wes. Rumor has it I can be bossy."

His gaze studied mine, his eyes crinkling at the corners when he smiled again. "I don't mind that."

I felt so flustered inside, heat blooming from my chest outward and climbing up my neck into my cheeks. "So, uh, I'll go. Today's Friday..." I paused. I could be the queen of obvious sometimes. "So tomorrow? Maybe we could take a drive to Anchorage with Ross for pet shopping."

"I think that's perfect. We'll make it a thing. I'll have to figure out who's gonna watch Nilla while we're gone."

"I'll ask Alice. She'll be happy to help."

Chapter Eight

WES

Ross blinked up at me, and my chest hurt. Maybe I hadn't seen his dad in person in over two years, but I had continued to count George as one of my closest friends. We'd been in touch via text several times a week and chatted when we played online games together. Every time I looked into Ross's eyes, it stung a little. They were so much like his father's.

"Okay," Ross said slowly. "Where will Nilla go?"

"We're dropping her off at a friend's place," I said.

I was relieved Tiffany had thought ahead. She was going to be here any minute, and then we would drive over together to drop Nilla off at Alice and Jonah's place.

"There's a lake and everything there," I added.

"She'll be okay?" Ross prompted.

"Absolutely. Alice is a veterinarian."

He eyed me skeptically before nodding his approval. "That's cool." He looked over at Nilla, who thumped her tail on the floor.

A short while later, Ross was in the back seat with Nilla, and Tiffany was in the passenger seat beside me as I drove toward Alice and Jonah's house. "You work with Jonah, right?" she prompted.

"Yup. Alice's grandmother Bea is a friend of my mom's too."

"If you haven't been to their place, it's on one of the glacier lakes. It's a tiny lake, but it's beautiful," Tiffany added.

"Is it frozen?" Ross's voice reached us from the back seat. Tiffany had offered to let him ride in the front, but he'd wanted to be in the back with Nilla.

Tiffany turned in her seat, glancing over her shoulder. She rested her arm on the edge of the seat as she angled to look at Ross. "It is frozen. Come summer, we can take Nilla there and she can go swimming with Alice's dog."

After we dropped Nilla off, I caught myself stealing glances at Tiffany again and again while we drove to Anchorage. I kept absorbing little details about her. The tiny freckles on her cheeks, the way the wind tousled her hair when she asked to crack the windows even though it was cold out. When Ross started asking curious questions about the mountains and the glaciers, Tiffany provided him with a running commentary. She promised to take him to the town's transfer station for the "best eagle viewing," and he was thrilled.

Once we arrived at the pet store, Tiffany glanced down at Ross. "Okay, have at it. Should we make it a race?"

Ross blinked up at her, a furrow forming between his brows. "A race?"

She waggled her eyebrows with a mischievous glint in her eyes. "That's right. I get a cart, you get a cart, and..." Her eyes slid to me, and I tried to ignore the sizzle of electricity crackling in the air between us.

"Wes might go for it. We have ten minutes to see how much we can get."

A look of glee entered Ross's eyes as he smiled up at her. "Yes!"

Before I had a chance to offer any feedback on this plan, they were grabbing carts and dashing through the store. I snagged a cart, jogging alongside Tiffany. "You're crazy," I offered.

She grinned at me. "No, I'm not. He needs some fun, and this is a thing the store does. You have ten minutes, and it's only a hundred bucks for whatever you get, not counting the food. You're in charge of the food."

I hustled over to the food section, stocking up quickly on treats and food. When I turned out of the aisle, Tiffany and Ross were neck and neck in a race for the checkout.

Tiffany threw her hands up in the air, letting her cart roll forward as they reached the registers. When I caught up and looked toward Ross, I understood exactly why she did that. It was fun, and he needed something silly. His smile was wide and the sort of numb look in his eyes had disappeared.

I stopped behind them. "Who is the official winner?"

The guy at the register grinned as he glanced over at us, thumbing toward Ross. "Maybe by a foot."

Tiffany lifted her hand, slapping it to Ross's palm. "Rock on, dude. Maybe we should sign you up for track when it starts."

"Track?" Ross prompted as the guy began ringing us up.

"Running. Did you do any sports before?" she asked.

"Soccer," he offered.

"Do you want to play soccer this spring?" I asked.

When Ross glanced uncertainly back and forth between us, my heart gave a painful squeeze that was becoming familiar. Even though we had both known his parents, we didn't know him that well, and we weren't familiar with his childhood.

"Okay," he said with a quick dip of his chin.

Tiffany slid her arm around his narrow shoulders, her palm curling over his upper arm and sliding up and down in a comforting gesture. Somehow, we were in charge of this kid. Ready or not.

After we loaded everything in the car and piled back into my SUV, Tiffany suggested we get lunch. A few minutes later, we were seated at a table at a burger place. Her knee brushed against mine. A layer of denim and the fleece from her leggings was between us, and I was still acutely aware of the subtle touch.

Her eyes caught mine, and it was all I could do not to lean over and kiss her. Her mouth was—well, I paid way too much attention to the plumpness of her bottom lip, the way her lips curled at the corners when she began to smile, and the way she had a habit of biting the corner of her lip, just two teeth denting the plush surface.

I forced myself to look away. I glanced out the window of the café, commenting, "It's clouding up. Looks like snow."

Tiffany chatted with Ross, asking him questions about his favorite classes as she explained he would start school next week in Willow Brook. When we walked out after lunch, she took a deep breath and glanced at Ross. "It smells like snow."

"Snow smells?" he asked, looking up at her curiously.

She nodded. "I forgot all about how snow smells

when I lived away from here for a few years. It's the quality of the air. It smells good, kind of crisp. I don't know how else to explain it." She looked over at me. "Do you know what I mean?"

I breathed in the snow-scented air, nodding as I smiled over at her, my pulse revving like a restless engine. "I do." Looking at Ross, I added, "You'll see. After it snows a few times, you'll know what we mean."

Light snow began to fall as we drove home, but it quickly grew heavier. I glanced at Tiffany. "Was a storm supposed to come in?"

Her worried eyes bounced from me to the view out the windows. "It was a twenty percent chance when I checked my weather app this morning. It didn't say it was going to snow like this, though."

Ross straightened, leaning forward to look out the window. "Wow. I've never seen it snow like this."

By the time we exited the highway for Willow Brook, visibility was poor. Ross was worried about Nilla. Having grown up in Alaska, I was accustomed to driving in bad weather, but I was relieved Alice and Jonah lived on the way to my place.

I glanced at Tiffany, and as if she read my mind, she offered, "I've already texted Alice. She'll walk up to the road and meet us."

In short order, we had picked up Nilla and drove to my house. After we unloaded the new pet supplies and Ross took Nilla out for a walk, I looked over at Tiffany.

"I don't think you should drive in this," I said.

She spun around. "You just drove us here. Are you serious?"

I gestured to the windows. "I kept driving because we were already on the road. I wouldn't choose to go back out. There's like zero visibility, Tiffany. I'm just relieved we got here. How far is your place from here?"

"About fifteen minutes."

"In good weather?" I prompted.

She rolled her eyes, but nodded. "Fine I'll stay here."

Chapter Nine

WES

A few hours later, Ross was sound asleep in his bedroom with Nilla on the foot of his bed. With a little help from my mother, I'd gotten bedding for the spare bedroom for him last night. I wanted him to be able to pick out his own stuff, but that could wait.

I felt as if the universe had set out to torture me. I'd been battling my arousal for hours by this point. Spending time with Tiffany in close quarters had short-circuited my discipline and willpower. She was standing in the kitchen while my eyes were lingering on the curve of her hips.

I had started a fire in the woodstove, which was all fine and well, except it made the house hot. She had stripped out of her jacket and the flannel shirt she wore over her tank top. Turning, she was drying her hands on a dish towel when she looked over at me.

"I wasn't prepared to stay over. I hope you have a spare toothbrush or something," she said.

"Well, you got a whole pack of toothbrushes for Wes, so you can use one of those," I offered, thinking this was a safe topic.

She draped the towel over the oven handle and walked over to where I stood by the counter, my hand curled on the edge. She rested her hip against it and crossed her arms. Not a helpful move because her arms plumped her breasts up slightly. My eyes had a mind of their own and dipped down, lingering on the curves. I wanted to trail my fingertips over her skin. Hell, I wanted to drag my tongue into the valley between her breasts and tease her ruched nipples.

She cleared her throat, and I lifted my eyes. Her cheeks were flushed pink. We studied each other. "Wes..." she began. She gave her head a little shake, biting her bottom lip.

My cock throbbed in response. "Yes?" I prompted.

She muttered something, followed with, "Fuck it."

The next thing I knew, her arms unfolded, and she stepped closer, staring up at me. I felt as if she were daring me.

"What are you doing?" I rasped.

"This is crazy. This whole situation is crazy," she said, throwing her hands up as she took another step closer.

I could feel the heat of her body, and her breasts pressed against my chest. "What's crazy?" I could barely hear my own voice over the thundering beat of my heart. My need was tightening, digging spurs into my side, urging my pulse faster and faster.

"Well, we're guardians to Ross. I know we're not technically his parents, but for all intents and purposes, we are because his parents are gone." She blinked quickly, sadness and pain flashing in her eyes. "So there's that, and then this."

Before I could ask what *this* was, she leaned up, sliding a hand around the back of my neck, and pulled me down. Her mouth met mine. It literally felt as if lightning cracked through the air, loud and fiery enough to cleave a tree in half. In this case, the electricity crackled into the fire simmering on low burn inside me and it burst into flames.

I palmed her cheek and slid an arm around her waist, bringing her body flush against mine. I couldn't hold back the growl of satisfaction in the back of my throat when I angled my head to the side and her mouth opened with a gasp. The feel of her tongue gliding against mine was heaven.

Tiffany kissed boldly. One of her hands landed on my low back, just under the hem of my T-shirt. I could feel the press of every fingertip against my skin sending sparks leaping into the bonfire burning between us.

My hand slid down to cup her bottom, that bottom I'd been thinking about since the first time we encountered each other at the shelter months ago. Even then, I had wanted her. She was so fucking sensual and sexy, carrying this earthy bold quality to her that called to me.

She rocked her hips against mine. My arousal was unmistakable. I was hot and hard, and I wanted her, all of her, right now.

Her tongue teased against mine before she abruptly broke free. We stared at each other. My palm slid from her cheek to the side of her neck where I could feel the rapid beat of her pulse just beneath my thumb. Her nipples were tight and pressed against my chest.

"Oh fuck," she whispered.

Chapter Ten

TIFFANY

Wes's eyes held mine, dark and heavy-lidded. I was trying to breathe, trying to get my pulse to slow down. All to no avail. A distant part of my brain recognized I was seeking a distraction from the startling loss of my friend and being thrown into responsibility for her son.

Wes was the perfect distraction. I wanted him to a point of feeling near frantic. I could feel the slick arousal at the apex of my thighs and the hard ridge of his cock cradled against my low belly.

I tried to catch my breath, but my heart kept on racing. It felt like sparks were dancing across the surface of my skin. Wes studied me, and I didn't like the prickle of uncertainty I felt inside.

Although it took every ounce of my willpower to do it, I forced myself to step back. The sound of my swallow was audible.

"What was that about?" he finally asked, his voice holding an edge of huskiness.

Dear God. All this man had to do was speak and I wanted him even more. My channel clenched and I shifted on my feet, attempting to relieve the pressure building there.

My face felt like it was on fire. "I wanted to kiss you," I finally said, lifting my chin and holding his gaze.

I watched as he took a breath, his shoulders rising with it. He hooked a thumb in the pocket of his jeans. My gaze dropped to his forearm, muscled and dusted with dark hair. My eyes trailed down to his hand. He had strong, capable hands, the kind that could get a job done. I wanted his touch on me, on my bare skin.

"I wanted to kiss you too," he said bluntly.

My eyes whipped up, caught instantly in the beam of his.

"Ever since we met again. When you came to the shelter with Alice," he added.

Before I could think better of it, I was honest. "I wanted to kiss you then too." I bit my lip, feeling abashed and wishing I could take the words back. "We can't be stupid about this."

"No, we can't," he agreed.

———

Somehow, I stumbled through the rest of the conversation with Wes. He insisted I take the bed in his bedroom. Ross had wanted to stay in the guest room because he said it was his, so Wes had gotten the daybed made up for him.

I had tried to argue the point, but Wes sort of glowered at me. I acquiesced because it seemed silly to do otherwise.

My sleep was restless. I couldn't stop thinking about the feel of Wes's body pressed close against mine. He was built, seriously built. And the way he held me was so strong with a touch of commanding, but not overbearing, not overpowering. *Just so.* Sometime in the darkness, I awoke, again, with the sheets tangled around me.

I was still aroused, my nipples taut peaks and slick heat at my core. I finally gave in to the need rushing through me. I was in Wes's bed, the scent of him surrounding me—earthy with a touch of salt and crisp, like the ocean. I was certain many men smelled like the outdoors, but Wes's scent had an appeal that called to me on an elemental level.

I'd fallen asleep in my tank top and panties. My hands coasted down over my breasts, one dipping under the elastic of my panties. I bit my lip, trying to hold back the moan that escaped when my fingers slipped into my dripping wet folds.

I must've dreamed about Wes. As it was, I'd gone to sleep unbearably aroused and flustered by our kiss. It was as if the kiss had only happened moments ago because my body was ready to detonate at nothing more than a touch of my own fingers. I closed my eyes, imagining his mouth on mine again and his fingers in place of my own.

I was ready, so fucking ready. I teased my fingers around my clit, and my climax came abruptly. I shuddered with one hand buried between my thighs and the other clenching the sheets as tremors rippled through my body.

Chapter Eleven

WES

My house was small, and I'd never been so acutely aware of just how small it was as I listened to Tiffany. I was sleeping on the couch in the living room. I'd been restless for hours.

Fuck me. That kiss had made me almost lose my fucking mind. Listening to her whimper and moan followed by the sound of her release nearly pushed me beyond my limits. I knew she had no idea I could hear her.

Meanwhile, my cock was the equivalent of a tire rod in my briefs. I kicked off the blanket and strode into the bathroom. Moments later, I found my own release in the shower, my head hanging in relief that at least the tension was gone. My hand was a poor substitute for what I knew it would be like with Tiffany, but I had to get some sleep.

The following morning, snow blanketed the ground. Ross was thrilled to take Nilla outside to play. I was standing by the living room windows, a mug of coffee in hand, as I watched them cavort. My mom tended to view most events through a spiritual lens.

She had already said she thought Nilla came to me because Ross needed her. She was right on that score. Pondering how Ross might be doing without Nilla was almost painful to contemplate.

Ross was kicking snow up in the air while Nilla leaped into the falling snow and watched while he attempted to make a few snowballs. The dry and fluffy snow didn't make the best snowballs, but Nilla didn't care. She was a dog and had a little boy fully focused on her. My heart squeezed tight.

At the sound of motion, I turned to see Tiffany coming out of the bathroom. Her cheeks were flushed pink, and her hair was damp from her shower. I ignored the flare of heat rising inside.

"Good morning," I said. "Coffee's ready."

She looked at me from across the room, and the flush on her cheeks deepened. Every cell in my body fired in reaction.

"Good morning," she replied huskily.

We stood there staring at each other, probably for too long. Whether or not we ever admitted it to each other, I was pretty sure she knew I had found my release in the shower last night while I was aware she'd found hers in my bed.

I cleared my throat. "If you're hungry, I can make some scrambled eggs."

She studied me for another moment before her lips kicked up just a tiny bit. "That would be nice."

We ended up having what ranked as the most domestic morning of my adult life. I made scrambled eggs while Ross sat at the table with Nilla lying by his feet. The three of us ate together, and Tiffany helped clean up.

She left after that. Even though I wanted to kiss her again, I didn't.

Afterward, I looked over at Ross, wondering what to do. Blessedly, despite the gaping loss he'd just experienced, he seemed mostly okay. I had enough sense to know his well-being was shaky at best, though.

"You don't have to worry about entertaining me. I can play outside with Nilla or..." His eyes twinkled. "We can play video games."

I burst out laughing. "We could do both."

And we did. All the while, I wondered when I would see Tiffany again.

Chapter Twelve

TIFFANY

I *loved* a list. I used lists for everything. The following day, I sat down and wrote one.

Don't kiss Wes again.

Don't think about kissing Wes again.

Definitely don't think about what else you could do with Wes.

I folded the piece of paper and put it in my office desk drawer.

"Hey, you got a sec?" Alice called from down the hall.

"I always have time for you," I said as I stood from the desk, walking briskly down the hallway. When I peered into the exam room where she was, Alice was holding a corgi and cast me a rueful glance.

"He looked really sweet when he came in," she commented.

"What's up, Bowtie?" I asked the corgi who had been the picture of joy and cheer when he came into the waiting area a mere fifteen minutes ago. His eyes were wide, and he looked furious.

The owner was crying. She looked up at me,

sobbing, "He gets so upset about getting his nails trimmed."

"Oh, are we breaking your heart?" I asked as I approached Bowtie, aptly named by the white marking on the back of his neck shaped like a bow tie.

I looked over at his owner, who blew her nose in a tissue. "We are in the process of hiring a vet tech," I shared.

Alice arched one brow. "I don't know how much that's going to help with this guy. His legs are so short there's nothing to get ahold of, and his body is a tube. He's all muscle." She looked over at the owner, offering helpfully, "I'm so glad he's in good shape."

The woman snorted at that.

Alice was sitting on the floor with Bowtie and scratched behind his ears. "If it's okay with you, we can give him something for his anxiety. This is anxiety-based aggression. It's really stressing him out. We can give him medication and let him chill out with you, then try to cut his nails in a bit."

The owner nodded vigorously. "I'm on board!"

"There are other ways to go about this, but his anxiety is so severe, I don't want to make it worse. My prediction would be if he comes for vet appointments a few times with some anxiety assistance, his fear will resolve because the experience will be good instead of terrifying."

The owner waited with Bowtie in the exam room after he took the medication, and Alice and I walked out front together. I smiled over at her. "You're good."

She laughed under her breath. "Bowtie doesn't want his nails clipped. It's scary. We can do some behavioral strategies and training later, but first, we need to get him not to be terrified. What's the rest of my day look like?" Pausing beside my desk, she added, "I need a pen."

She opened the desk drawer before my brain caught up. The list I had folded up was sitting on top, and the motion of her opening the drawer caused it to unfold. I stayed quiet, my pulse racing a little as I prayed Alice didn't notice it. She snagged a pen and went to close the drawer. I let out a silent sigh of relief.

My luck ran out because the paper unfolded even more and was caught in the edge of the drawer. It fell on the floor. Alice leaned down, picking it up. "What's this?" she asked curiously as she looked down.

Heat crawled up my neck and into my cheeks. "Nothing," I said a little too brightly.

She looked from the list to me, her lips curling in a sly smile. "Are we kissing Wes now?" She handed me the list.

"Not anymore," I said firmly as I folded the list twice.

"I like Wes," she stated. "He was so nice at the shelter. He's on the same crew as Chase and Jonah at work. They both say he's great."

"Oh right," I said all casually as if I wasn't trying to surreptitiously absorb every nugget of information I could about this man.

I crossed over to the shredder and dropped the list in, immediately hitting the button and listening to the quick vroom of the machine. My list was shredded into tiny scraps. Good riddance. Maybe the universe was telling me to let go of my love of lists.

"You don't have any more appointments today." I crossed my arms and lifted my eyes to the clock. "In fact, now that you've given Bowtie anxiety medication, you'll end up being late, and Jonah will wonder where you are."

Alice gave me a sideways look, just as her dog, the very dog she found at the shelter where I'd encountered Wes for the first time since high school, sidled closer to her. She leaned over to stroke her palm down Honey's back as she glanced back up at me. "Jonah is working out at the station. He doesn't usually keep tabs on my schedule," she said pointedly. "I told him I'd pick up a pizza. Why don't you go with me? I'll bring some home for him, and you can tell me why you're kissing Wes and refuse to date anyone."

Alice was quiet for the first few minutes while we ate. We were dining at Alpenglow Pizza, a newer place in Willow Brook that had quickly become popular for its woodfired pizza. They had some fancier options, but I often defaulted to the basics. I'd needed stress relief, so I ordered double pepperoni with extra cheese.

After I finished a slice, Alice took a sip of water and cocked her head to the side as she studied me. "Okay, explain." She circled her hand in the air.

"There's nothing to explain," I said quickly. "I kissed Wes, but it was totally a mistake. Just like my list said, it won't happen again. We have to focus on Ross."

"Obviously, Ross is a priority, but kissing Wes doesn't change that. Also, that's not all I'm asking about, and you know it. We've gotten close since you started working for me. You are *all* about making sure everybody else finds love and all that."

"Hey, I only made sure you did. Plus, you and Jonah are perfect for each other," I pointed out.

Alice narrowed her eyes, taking none of my bullshit. "Ha! As soon as you get a chance to set someone else up or decide they're dating the right person, you'll be all over that shit. You are as bad as Bea." She was referring to Jonah's grandmother, a seriously nosy busybody, and an unabashed matchmaker.

"So what? I *love* love. Bea is thrilled that you and Jonah are together. Even you have to admit, you two are working out just great. Your mood has been much better since you've been getting it on the regular."

She snorted and took a swallow of water. Her assessing gaze coasted over my face, and I willed myself not to squirm.

She circled her hand in the air again. "Just tell me, Tiffany. It's fine if you just want to be alone, but I feel like there's more to the story."

I wrinkled my nose and pressed my glasses up as I considered my friend. For as nice as Alice was, she had an implacable stubborn streak. It rarely showed itself. In fact, the only time I'd seen it surface was in relation to caring for animals and making sure the people she cared about were okay. While I appreciated being in the pool of people who Alice counted as a friend who mattered, just this second, I was annoyed. Because I knew she was going to patiently wait until I finally explained.

I let out of breath and took a quick sip of my water. "Fine. I have to give you credit for your patience anyway." She cocked her head to the side, arching a brow. "So do you remember my mom?"

Alice looked a little confused but nodded. "Of course. You look a lot like her. You're beautiful."

"That was a sideways compliment," I muttered, annoyance pricking me. Not annoyance with Alice, but the fact that I looked like my mother.

"Well, she *was* beautiful. So are you. I don't even remember what she did."

In the small world of Willow Brook and the locals born and raised here, it was rare not to know at least something about someone and what they did, even if you didn't know them well. That was the thing about my mom. She'd never had a stable job. She was always coming and going.

"She was..." I paused, shrugging. "Restless, I suppose."

"I know she passed away, and you almost never speak of her," Alice said gently.

Alice's parents had died in a boating accident. I remembered her parents. They'd always seemed, well, happy in a comfortable way. And stable, the opposite of my mother. I thanked the universe, the stars, and God many times that my father had been as solid as a rock, just a steady guy. He still was.

"How did she die?" she asked.

"Cancer. The sad thing is, after spending most of my childhood desperate to get my mother to love me, to stay in one place and be stable, I was kind of relieved when she passed away. Which sounds awful, I know. We had a complicated relationship, I guess you could say."

Alice reached across the table, one of her hands curling over mine. She squeezed gently. I didn't even realize how cold my hands were until I felt the contrast of her touch. She released her grip, dipping her chin. "It's okay. We don't get to choose our parents."

"No, we certainly don't." I took a breath, steeling myself. "Anyway, aside from her not being the most stable person, Chase and I watched her treat my dad like shit. It took me a long time to realize that he ignored it. He's never said it, but I think he basically made a deal with himself that he had committed to us, and that was all that mattered to him. At least as far as our family was concerned. And my mom? She was always chasing after something. She wanted to be a model, then an actress, then in a band, and she bounced around trying to find work. She had two affairs. One of them with..." I paused, unsure if I should even say the name, hesitating just long enough that all I offered was, "One of my high school teachers."

My heart stung with the burn of it, remembering how desperately I craved my mother's attention. Emotionally speaking, she'd never been an available parent for Chase or me. She had even viewed me as her competition somehow as I got older. I'd borne more of the brunt of her flashes of irritation and this rage that you felt more than you saw. She kept it bottled up tightly. It would flash like lightning in the darkness sometimes. I always felt like my relationship with my mother was like the surface of a lake. There was what was visible to the eye and what was hidden underneath, teeming with things I still didn't understand.

Realizing Alice was waiting for me to continue, I sucked in a breath before explaining, "So yeah, I didn't grow up with a great model for healthy relationships. As awesome as my dad has been, I guess it almost made me more cynical. I felt like it shouldn't have turned out that way for him. He deserved better, and it didn't matter anyway."

I paused to take another bite of pizza, grateful for the ridiculous amount of cheese and pepperoni. The flavors soothed me. After I finished chewing, I cocked my head to the side, fiddling with my napkin and folding it into a tidy triangle again and again as I began to talk. "I dated here and there, but I never really trusted anyone enough to get serious." I rolled my eyes. "I didn't have a single serious relationship in college, and the sex was nothing to celebrate."

Alice's lips twitched at the corners. "Ah, well, it can be better," she offered lightly.

I snorted, needing the humor to bolster me. "I had a good friend in college, Scott. We got close. Before I knew it, we kind of slid into this friends-with-benefits situation after we graduated." I shrugged. "We started to have feelings for each other. He said something about it first, and we decided to be exclusive. I thought maybe I had found a way to avoid all the things I worried about." I swept my hand in a small arc in the air. "Because I knew him. We'd been friends since freshman year. He was the reason I stayed down there. I also got a good job. The place where I worked in HR before I moved home." I paused, hesitating to continue.

My friend nodded encouragingly, and I forced myself to keep talking. "Then I had a scare. I'm fine," I said firmly. "But I had to have surgery to remove what turned out to be a benign nerve tumor. Scott didn't even reply to my text."

Alice's eyes widened. "What do you mean? Did he not know what happened? Since you're sitting in front of me and apparently okay, we won't dwell on that now, but I want more info."

I let out a bitter laugh. "I'll fill you in. Yeah, he knew. I called him as soon as I was referred to oncology because they didn't know if it was benign. He was all freaked out. I could tell. I'm not sure what he thought. They ran some tests, and I wanted him to go with me to the follow-up appointment. He dumped me instead. By text. Then he ghosted me completely."

There was still a scorched burn on my heart. It felt as if my heart was a building, and a car had crashed into the corner, damaging it badly but leaving the rest standing. I'd walled off that corner.

"Oh my God," Alice breathed. "What a fucking asshole."

My friend's gray eyes were dark and stormy looking. I knew she would go to battle for me. I didn't need it anymore, but it still felt good.

I rolled my eyes, twisting my lips to the side. "Yeah, he's a total fucking asshole. Anyway, to clarify what happened, it turned out to be benign, so I'm fine. The jerk had the nerve to call me to check in like a month later after completely ghosting me. When I told him everything would be fine, he tried to apologize. I told him to fuck off. When someone can't be there when it matters, you know you don't really matter. After the fact, I found out I wasn't his only friend with benefits. Another mutual friend of ours from college reached out to me later. She knew the whole thing. She just wanted me to know he pulled the same kind of bullshit with her, acting like she was special and saying he wanted to be exclusive. He never was. She found out about me *and* some other woman. I just decided romance wasn't worth it. I have enough trust issues to begin with. I don't really need it. You know, statistically speaking, the happiest people are older women who are single and don't have kids."

Alice had just taken a sip of her water. She sputtered, her eyes wide as she looked over at me.

I grinned. "True story. Look it up."

She dabbed at her mouth with a napkin while I

grabbed another one and wiped up the water on the table in front of her.

"You know, I'm sure that is true because you're all about the research and the facts, but happiness is complicated. For fuck's sake, Scott's a real asshole. I bet that did a number on your sense of trust."

"Yeah. It was already shaky at best. Aside from friends and my dad and my brother, I don't really trust people, not when it comes to romance."

"You were so into me going for it with Jonah. What was that about?"

My heart burned. "I guess I believe in it for other people, just not me. Plus, Jonah is a good guy."

"Don't you think Wes is a good guy?" she asked pointedly, even pursing her lips for good measure as she pinned me with her sharp, knowing gaze.

"Sure," I replied with a shrug. "But it's not worth the risk."

I was being honest with Alice, but I couldn't tell her how terrifying it was to think about trusting anyone. After the humiliation and pain I'd experienced with the way Scott blew me off, I couldn't handle it.

"Wes *is* a good guy," I emphasized. "But he and I have other priorities right now. We can't go around kissing each other." I took a breath, thinking of Ross and his parents. "I mean, Ross lost both of his parents."

Alice's eyes were soft as she looked over at me. "He did, and he's blessed to have you two. You'll be a great mom."

"Um, I'm not his mom."

"Maybe not biologically, but you are. I know you're technically his guardian, but you and Wes are his parents. You can get all hung up on the legal defini-tion, but you're the ones doing the whole thing. You don't do anything half-ass, especially not love." Alice paused, studying me. "And that's how I know just how shitty what Scott did was. You don't do anything by half measures, not at all. You cared about him, and he tossed you away like nothing. Fucking asshole," she said vehemently.

Blessedly, Alice let the topic drop then. That was about all I could handle. We finished eating our pizza. As we walked out into the crisp, cold night, we stopped at our cars together, and she glanced over at me.

"I'm looking forward to hearing just how long you hold out from kissing Wes." She snickered when I glared at her.

"Nice to meet you," the assistant principal, who'd asked me to call her Ms. Dana, said.

"You as well," I replied, reaching to clasp her proffered hand.

Ms. Dana smiled, gesturing to the table after we shook hands. "Have a seat. You must be Ross." She turned her attention to Ross, who stood beside me.

My hand was resting between his shoulder blades. Even though he was putting on a brave face, I knew he was nervous. I could feel the anxiety emanating from him.

He blinked up at her. "I am."

"Well, I'm Ms. Dana. It's very nice to meet you. We're here to talk about your classes. You can sit beside Wes."

We both sat down at the table. "Tiffany should be here any..." I began, just as I heard the sound of footsteps moving briskly down the hallway.

I recognized the rhythm of Tiffany's stride. I felt my body humming and tightening with anticipation. A moment later, she appeared in the doorway. My gaze took her in. She was wearing a silky blue blouse with a scoop neck and a bow nestled at the valley of her breasts. Of course, my greedy eyes lingered on the hint of exposed curves. Her silvery-gray down jacket was unzipped. Her jeans were fitted and tucked into a pair of cowboy boots. I wanted to peel off all of her clothes.

The sound of someone clearing their throat snapped my eyes away from Tiffany.

"Hi," Tiffany said brightly. She smiled over at the assistant principal. "Nice to see you again." She glanced at Ross. "I knew Ms. Dana when we were kids and saw her last week when she brought her cat to the vet."

Ms. Dana smiled. "Rumple did better with Alice than any of the temporary vets. He still meowed as if he was being killed, but he was just fine after his shots."

Tiffany grinned. "Alice is fantastic."

Tiffany sat down on the other side of Ross, and I sensed she felt as protective as I did.

Ms. Dana sat across from us, opening a laptop. "Let's look at his class schedule. I'm also wondering if you can help us get the records from his last school."

Tiffany jumped in. "Of course. We have all the paperwork to do that."

The meeting was fairly routine, I suppose. I'd never been to a school meeting, and I felt like I was floundering. When Ross was at the house, I thought I was doing okay with the parenting thing. He would eat just about anything, with cereal and pizza as his top choices. Conveniently, I loved both as well. We also enjoyed some of the same video games. He mostly played sports, and liked racing video games, which was handy because I felt like those were in the safe category for kids.

At the end of the meeting, Ms. Dana escorted us out to the main hallway. She planned to walk Ross to his homeroom and let us know we were free to go. Apparently, we both had to go to the bathroom because Tiffany asked, "Can you tell me where the restroom is?" just as I chimed in, "Restroom?"

Ms. Dana nodded. "Down the hallway and around the corner." She gestured to the side. "It's right back there. You can go out the back door from there into the parking area. It's an exit-only door."

Without speaking about it, we waited together while Ross walked down the hallway with her. Tiffany caught my eyes when they disappeared around a corner, mouthing, "He'll be fine."

As we turned and walked toward the restroom, I was hyperaware of Tiffany's presence at my side. I had replayed our kiss in my thoughts more times than I would admit to anyone, even myself.

I gestured to the doorway. "You first." She stepped into the bathroom. We were tucked out of sight in this short hallway with only the door to the bathroom visible.

A moment later at the sound of the door opening, I glanced over to see Tiffany stepping out. She stood in front of me, adjusting her purse strap on her shoulder. Her tongue swiped across her bottom lip. I had to take a quick breath. Fuck. *This* woman. She fiddled with the strap of her purse, her hand curling tightly around it.

"So, uh, do we want to have dinner together with Ross?" she asked. "I called the therapist Eileen recommended, and she said it would be good if we came together for his first appointment. Would you do that?"

"Of course. Just tell me when. Ross loves pizza." My words felt out of place for a second, but I added quickly, "For dinner, we could do that. Maybe tonight?"

She nodded. "Why don't you guys come to my place? We can get takeout. It's an apartment downtown. I've got his room all set."

"Sounds like a plan."

We stood there, and the silence started to feel awkward. "I need to go to the bathroom, if you don't mind," I finally said.

"Okay, I'll text you."

When I stepped into the bathroom, I closed the door and leaned against it for a moment. I had to pee, and I had a hard-on. *That* wasn't the most comfortable thing. I was relieved I had to force myself through it because my damn erection went away.

I washed my hands quickly and stepped out, surprised to see Tiffany still standing there.

"We forgot to say what time." She paused, sliding her tongue over her bottom lip again. I was starting to wonder if she was trying to torture me. "And I needed to say something." Her words came out in a rush.

"Uh, sure. What's that?"

She took a deep breath, pushing her shoulders back. I swear to God, it felt like we had a physical force between us. When her teeth sank into her bottom lip, my balls tightened.

She didn't say anything for several beats, and I watched as a flush crested on her cheeks. Before I knew it, we were stepping closer together. She opened her mouth to say something. I felt her fingers curl into my shirt when she said, "Fuck it."

She arched up as I bent low to meet her. When our lips collided, it felt as if lightning flashed around us. Her mouth was soft and lush, and I savored the way she instantly opened for me.

Her tongue darted out to tease against mine. I wasn't thinking when I nudged her back, pressing my palms against the wall on either side of her as if it was too much to let my hands touch her. As it was, our bodies were plastered together. My arousal was cradled against her low belly. Our kiss went on and on and on.

We broke apart swiftly at the sound of footsteps, staring at each other. I moved back and stepped to the door that led outside. "Come on."

We walked outside just as someone came around the corner in the hallway. The icy-cold air struck my cheeks. We walked briskly toward our vehicles. When we stopped behind them, I commented, "You parked beside me."

She nodded, staring up at me. "We can't kiss like that," she blurted.

I studied her. Something like fear and a deep worry flickered in her gaze. Protectiveness rose swiftly inside. I wanted to encircle her, to hold her close and tell her everything would be okay when I didn't even know what exactly was wrong.

"Tiffany..." I began.

She held a palm up. "I can't talk about this. I have to go."

Before I could say anything else, she dashed past me, climbed into her car, and started it. She rolled down her window as she was backing out and called out, "I'll text you what time. See you tonight."

Chapter Fifteen

TIFFANY

"Hey there," Hallie called as I walked into the kitchen.

My sister-in-law sat at the kitchen table in the house she shared with my brother, cradling their months-old baby boy in her arms. I paused beside her chair, sliding my arm around her shoulders and squeezing gently.

"Hey. He looks sound asleep." Danny was named after our father.

As I straightened, Hallie smiled up at me, her hazel eyes warm. "He is."

"Can I hold him?" I asked, my hands practically itching to hold my nephew.

Hallie nodded. "Absolutely."

"Will it wake him up?"

"When he's like this, if he wakes, he'll fall right back asleep."

She stood, carefully shifting Danny into my arms. The weight of their baby settled gently, and he molded against me as I adjusted him. His fist curled into his chin as he tucked his head into the curve of my shoulder.

Hallie stepped back, smiling. "I love him so much, but it's nice when someone else shows up to fuss over him."

I smoothed my hand over his silky soft hair. "I bet. I haven't had a baby myself, but I've seen how much work it is. Anytime you need a babysitter, just call. I feel like you don't ask for very much help."

My sister-in-law sat back down with a sigh, casting me a sheepish smile. "I never want to impose."

"Impose!"

"Chase is a huge help."

"My brother is the best kind of guy, and I'm so glad you two had that one-night stand."

Hallie's eyes went wide, and her cheeks flushed pink. My brother and Hallie had met like that, and she got pregnant because condoms weren't one hundred percent. Fortunately, they'd fallen in love, and now they had a baby. I was thrilled. My brother had been as cynical as me for years, maybe even more so.

I sat at the kitchen table as Hallie walked over to the counter, asking, "Would you like some coffee?"

"Yes, please."

She filled two mugs from the coffee pot. When she sat down across for me and handed a mug over, gesturing with one hand to the creamer on the table, she said, "It's fresh. I just made it before you got here. I missed coffee during my pregnancy."

She took a healthy swallow of her coffee, smiling as she let out a satisfied sigh and leaned back in her chair. Meanwhile, I looked down at my nephew. His lashes curled against his cheeks as he slept so deeply, and I envied him.

"Just a drop-in?" Hallie asked.

Looking up, I shrugged. I added cream to my

coffee with my free hand before I lifted the mug and took a swallow. "Yeah. I was over in this area."

"So get me up to speed. I'm all caught up on this guardianship situation. I've grilled Chase about Wes, by the way, and he assures me Wes is a solid guy. Both of you went to school with him, right?"

"We did. I think he was a few years ahead of me in Chase's grade. Honestly, I can't believe he's a firefighter, much less a hotshot firefighter."

"Why? Chase said he's great."

"It's just he was different in high school. He was kind of quiet and one of the smart kids." I felt my cheeks start to get hot.

"And what else is different?" My too-perceptive sister-in-law asked with a slight glint in her eyes.

"Well, he's hot. Not that he wasn't attractive in high school, I just didn't pay him much attention." I set my mug down as Hallie giggled.

She waggled her eyebrows. "Hot, huh?"

"Yeah," I returned, wishing my face didn't feel like it was on fire. "He's not a priority, though, because Ross is. The whole thing is a lot to take in. The attorney said we're to share guardianship unless one of us refuses. Neither one of us wants to refuse. I just hope it's okay for Ross. I've got a bedroom set up at my apartment. When Wes is out dealing with fires, he'll stay with me, and we'll figure it out."

"Maybe it's not the usual arrangement, but I think it's great. Obviously, Sarah and her husband trusted you two to make it work."

"Of course. I am a hundred percent there for Ross. I just hope this is the right move. There are so many what-ifs to worry about."

Hallie shook her head. "What if, what? It doesn't even matter. His parents died, and he needs both of you. I'm a firm believer that family is what you make of it. When you grow up, family is different. The idea expands and contracts. Like you're family to me now, and so are Chase and all the new friends I've made here in Willow Brook. I know it sounds cliché, but it does take a village to raise a child. I cannot imagine raising Danny without your help, without your dad, and without the various friends around me who have experience with babies and can give me advice when I panic.

"What weird things have happened?" I asked quickly.

"Nothing terrible. But Danny was congested one night, and I didn't know what to do, so Maisie stopped by and showed me how to do the trick with a bulb syringe. Sure, I could look online but having a human friend help is much better. I'd call you in the middle of the night if it was something serious, but I think you get my point."

"I do. Speaking of the family you make, I had a call with McKenna the other day, and she's planning to come for a visit soon. She said she texted you and Chase about it."

McKenna was my brother's half-sister. There'd been a mini bomb dropped in my family's life a few years ago. Our mother, the very one who'd screwed my head up around trust and commitment, had neglected to tell anyone that our father wasn't Chase's biological father. One of those handy ancestry websites had led Chase to discover his birth father and seven half-siblings. They were all awesome. I felt lucky because I'd always wanted a sister, and now I had one. Of the seven, there was only one girl. She was just as excited to have me, probably more so, than I was to discover her. Maybe we weren't even technically related, but she was my sister in every way that mattered.

Hallie nodded. "She did text. She said she and Rhys are coming by ferry to bring some stuff for the energy place." She waved a hand vaguely in the air.

"The part of their company Archer runs," I offered.

This half of Chase's family was very wealthy. You wouldn't know it to meet them, though. They were all down-to-earth and nice. Fireweed Industries was one of the most well-known companies in Alaska. It had started here and grown into an international consortium. The branch of the company here used to be a mine, but a friend who turned out to be Chase's cousin, Archer Cannon, had shut down the mine and turned it into a renewable resources business. They were expanding fast these days, which was great for Willow Brook because it brought in jobs.

"I'll make sure to text her so we have the dates. I'd love to have dinner." I paused, checking on Danny. He shifted in my arms and let out a soft sigh. I couldn't resist leaning down and nuzzling his cheek. Lifting my head, I smiled over at Hallie. "He smells so good. All soft and fresh."

"I know. That baby smell is magic. If it was possible to bottle it, I'm sure someone would make a fortune."

I nodded in agreement, smoothing my nephew's hair back. "Do you think it would be too much to bring Ross when McKenna and Rhys come for a visit?"

Hallie drummed her fingertips on the table before shrugging. "I don't think so. It's not like we're a wild group. I think the more he knows people are there for him, the better. Didn't you say the social worker set him up with a therapist here?"

I nodded. "I guess I'll ask her and see what she thinks. I'll also check with Wes."

I took a swallow of coffee as Hallie cocked her head to the side. "So aside from Wes being hot, how are you two handling this unexpected situation?"

"Okay, I guess. We're having pizza tonight at my place. It'll be Ross's first night there."

She leaped up from the table. "Wait a second," she called over her shoulder as she walked out of the kitchen and down the short hallway that led to the bedrooms. A moment later, she reappeared holding a box. "Chase got this for you," she announced as she placed it on the table and smoothed her hand over the surface.

"A PlayStation?" I looked up, a little confused.

"He said that Wes told him Ross likes playing video games. Chase already set up a subscription for him. Wes said they did the log-in and everything. With this, he can play at your place and save everything for when he's at Wes's. This way, he'll be able to do something he enjoys no matter where he is. Plus, it's leverage."

"Leverage?"

"Right now, he's probably just stunned. It won't be too long before he's a teenager, and this will give you leverage for discipline."

Ross's big brown eyes flashed in my thoughts, and my heart pinched. "I can't imagine having to discipline him."

"It'll happen eventually," she pointed out.

"I'll have to thank Chase. Actually, I'll do a voice text right now." I lifted my phone, tapping open the endless string of texts I shared with my brother before I tapped the microphone icon. "*Hey Chase, thanks for thinking of Ross and getting him the PlayStation. I'm sure he'll love it."*

I set the phone down after I hit send. "My video game skills are limited to what Chase taught me when we were younger."

Hallie lifted her hands and let them fall. "I don't even have those skills." We laughed together.

I left not much later. Glancing at the clock on my dashboard, I realized I would see Wes in just two hours. Anxiety tightened in my belly, and my pulse revved.

There were so many things to be nervous about. It was all complicated now that I totally had the hots for Wes, and he was a ridiculously good kisser. Gah! I wished he wasn't so good at it.

Scott, who'd ground my trust under the heel of his boot, had not been too good at kissing. I'd told myself it was worth it anyway. It wasn't. Not at all.

After I got home, I sent a text to Wes.

Me: *Chase has gifted Ross a PlayStation. I'm not that great at video games.*

Wes: *A PlayStation 5?*

Me: *I had to look at the box to see what you were talking about, but yes. Can you help set it up tonight?*

Wes: *Of course. I'll have to come over to your place a lot more to play. I don't have the PS5.* 😊

Me: *Chase told me you can set it up so that Ross can play at your place or mine.*

Wes: *Yup. I'm going to get Chase's gaming username. He can play with us.*

Me: *I think I'm the uncool guardian in this situation.*

Wes: *Nah, you're the coolest. You're a different kind of cool. If you want to learn how to play, I'll teach you.*

Me: *I can be a cheerleader, a couch cheerleader. Kind of like an armchair quarterback. Lol!*

Wes: *Just be you. What kind of pizza do you want?*

Me: *Pepperoni. They also have this amazing mushroom with smoked mozzarella and spinach. If you think you'll eat some, get that too. I'm not sure about Ross, though.*

Wes: *Maybe he'll be adventurous. I definitely want to try it. See you later.*

Our text exchange ended there, although my thumbs itched to keep this back-and-forth going.

It's just texting. You cannot get hot and bothered over Wes and texting.

But you are, my sly mind pointed out with a little glee.

"Yes!" Tiffany punched her fist in the air, being the couch cheerleader she'd promised.

Ross's online team was beating mine. I glanced over at her. "Whose team are you on?"

"I want you both to win," she insisted. "It's not my fault you guys decided to be on different teams. Since your team isn't winning, I'm rooting for Ross."

Ross grinned at her. My character had just died, so I had nothing to do. His thumbs moved rapidly on the controller as his eyes whipped back to the screen. "Let's be on the same team for the next game."

"I'm texting Chase. I'm gonna tell him to log in so we can play with him."

"Chase?" Ross prompted as he executed an expert dive and knocked out one of the other players on my team, which was losing badly at this point.

Tiffany answered. "My brother. The one who gave you this shiny new PS5."

"Oh right. I didn't remember that was his name."

"Hallie said they'd love to have us out for dinner soon. Would that be okay?" she asked.

I glanced over at Tiffany, willing my body not to react, but it was a lost cause. With her dark hair pulled up into a loose knot, she had a few curls dangling around her cheeks and along the nape of her neck. She was wearing glasses tonight, and I was discovering I had a weakness for her in glasses. Sexy as hell.

"Of course. I haven't been out to his place," I belatedly replied.

"Whenever we go, we can leave from here. I can drive, or you can."

Ross interjected, "I like Wes's SUV."

Tiffany shrugged. "Okay, but why?"

Ross glanced over, his lips curling at the corners. "Because it's cool."

"My car is cool," she protested even though it was obvious she wasn't the least bit offended.

Ross nodded in agreement. "Sure, but his is taller and it's black."

She chuckled. "If Wes doesn't mind driving, that's fine with me."

About two hours later, Tiffany cleared her throat, and I glanced over. "Yeah?"

She looked at her watch before her eyes shifted back to mine. "It's after ten."

"Ohhh," I said slowly. "Past bedtime." I wasn't used to paying attention to bedtime.

The reluctance emanating from Ross was powerful. Although, it was also obvious he was tired. Tiffany must have texted Chase because at that moment Chase said through the headset, "All right, guys, I gotta sign off. It's bedtime for me."

I knew I'd have to thank him later for that one. In short order, Ross did his bedtime routine. He brushed his teeth and changed without any prompting.

After he was in bed in the room Tiffany had set up

for him, I walked back down the short hallway to the living room and kitchen area. Tiffany's apartment looked out over Main Street in downtown Willow Brook.

"Nice little apartment," I commented as I glanced around.

"It's not a long-term place, but it works for now. I'm grateful there's a second bedroom."

Her apartment had hardwood floors and an angled ceiling with the kitchen to the back of the open area. A short hallway led to two bedrooms. One bathroom was off Tiffany's bedroom and the other was in the hallway.

"I had an idea," she said.

"What's that?"

"We can decorate Ross's bedroom at your place to match this one."

She had asked him what he wanted when we'd driven to Anchorage and somehow had already gotten it ready. It was a car-themed room fit for a middle schooler into race car games.

A slow grin tugged at the corners of my lips. "I like that idea. Just tell me where to order what you got, and I'll do it."

"I'll text you. I got it in Anchorage. I went back the day after we went with Ross." She waggled her eyebrows.

We were standing by the kitchen counter, and I could feel a magnetic pull to step closer to her. I rested my hand on the counter as if I could anchor myself in place there. She turned, resting her hips against the counter.

"The smoked mozzarella mushroom and spinach pizza was really good," I commented.

"It's one of my favorites."

"I'm not so sure Ross is into vegetables," I teased.

She grinned. "It's okay. That's not unusual for his age."

"I hated them all the way through high school, according to my mom. I had a cereal phase when that's all I ever wanted."

Tiffany's husky laughter sent a sizzle through my system. My eyes traced the winding path of one of the curls resting against her neck, shifting down to follow the collar of her blouse. The little bow at the center, just at the valley between her breasts, was unbearably tempting. It wasn't revealing, yet I felt my teeth clench. The temptation to lean down and untie that bow with my teeth was powerful

"Wes?" she prompted.

My eyes whipped up to hers, and I felt a little sheepish. The pink tinge staining her cheeks sent electricity sizzling through me. I didn't realize I had taken a step closer to her until I heard the soft intake of her breath.

"Wes," she began.

Her voice was a husky whisper. It was just her voice, for fuck's sake, yet I craved the sound of it. I let my gaze coast over her face—the subtle arch of her brows, the way her dark lashes curled against her cheeks when she blinked, the spray of freckles across the bridge of her nose and her cheeks, and the way her bottom lip was a little plumper than her top lip. When her tongue swiped across it, my body prickled with the imagined sensation of it because I wanted to feel her touch me.

I didn't mean to whisper her name. It was almost a growl, just a rasp of sound. I glanced down to see her hands curled on the edge of the counter. She was gripping it tightly. I watched as the flush on her cheeks deepened. Her mouth was parted slightly. I kept cataloging details about her—every single one of them was another match thrown in the fire of need, kindling the flames higher and higher.

"Wes?"

"Yes?"

"We can't kiss."

"Tell me why not." I heard myself saying.

Rational thought and reason had fled. Hell, they'd abandoned the building. The door to their return was locked firmly as need and desire threw a party in my body.

Tiffany worried her bottom lip as I waited, one hand gripping the counter.

"I don't know."

"We can be sensible," I offered, which was laughable. It was so ridiculous I couldn't believe I even suggested it.

"We need to focus on Ross," she pointed out quite sensibly.

"Don't you think we'll be able to think more clearly if we just get this out of our systems?"

Now *that* was an idea that made sense. I nodded to myself, almost proud for making that little point.

Her pretty blue eyes studied me. Her breath was a little unsteady, as was mine. She finally rolled her eyes, letting out a husky laugh. "I suppose that's something to consider."

"Only tonight," I said.

The sound of her swallow was audible. After several long beats, she nodded, just barely. I waited, holding myself in place. Because as fiercely as I desired her, I needed to know it was something she wanted.

Her hands uncurled from the counter, and she lifted one, tracing it along the stubbled edge of my jaw.

I turned to face her, putting both hands on the counter beside her hips. We stared at each other for several thundering heartbeats.

The air around us felt lit with a charge, heavy and weighted. In another moment, her hand slipped down the side of my neck and over my shoulder as she whispered, "Not fair."

"What's not fair?" I rasped.

Her eyes lifted to mine, a hint of mirth held in her gaze. "You're too hot."

Before I could reply, she leaned up and slid her hand around the back of my neck to pull me down to meet her mouth. That charge detonated, a lightning bolt sizzling between us when our lips met.

Her mouth opened instantly for me as she arched closer. I growled into her mouth at the feel of her soft curves pressing against me.

I had no idea how much time had passed. I could've kissed Tiffany for hours on end. The plush give of her lips, the teasing dance of her tongue with mine, and, fuck me, the little sounds she made—soft whimpers and husky pants when her mouth broke free from mine as we periodically needed to gasp for air before we fell back into kissing.

Like the rush of water tumbling down a mountainside, we started tugging at each other's clothes.

I let out a groan when my palm glided over Tiffany's soft skin. The curve of her belly felt just right. I brushed the backs of my knuckles along the plush softness of her breasts, savoring the sound of her moan when she broke away.

We stared at each other, our breath coming in rapid gasps. Her eyes had darkened to navy, and I saw my own need reflected in her gaze. With her lips parted slightly, her cheeks flushed a rosy shade of pink.

It felt as if every cell in my body was sizzling, the claws of need sinking deeper into me.

My eyes dipped down. Somewhere along the way, I'd unbuttoned her blouse. Her bra was black silk lace, her nipples tight and pressing against the fabric. I sucked in a breath, shackling my need. My hand had come to rest just on the side of her rib cage where I could feel the beat of her heart with every breath.

My gaze lifted to hers again. I tried to grasp some sort of rational thought that for some reason we shouldn't do this. Any chance of being rational had gone up in smoke in the midst of our kisses.

We studied each other, and I idly wondered if maybe she had more sense than me. She blinked, her teeth sinking into her bottom lip. The mere sight of that sent a shot of blood straight to my cock.

"Tell me we should stop," she said, her voice a husky rasp.

I sucked in a breath. "I was thinking maybe you should tell me that."

She worried her lip. The sight of her slightly crooked teeth denting the pink, plush surface nearly elicited a growl from me. That was how much I wanted her.

She released her lip, much to my chagrin, until the corner of her mouth curled up in a sly, teasing, sensual grin. It was almost a dare.

One of her palms was curled on the side of my hip, just under the hem of my shirt. She'd already unbut-toned my jeans and freed my cock. I felt the throb of it, hungry for her touch.

"You need to take your shirt off," she ordered.

I was excellent at following orders. From Tiffany, that was. I moved with alacrity, reaching behind my head and curling my fist around the back of my shirt before yanking it up and over my head. It fell to the floor. I didn't wait to slide my thumb under the clasp of her bra, nestled in the valley between her breasts. Seconds later, it snapped loose, and her breasts tumbled free. I closed the distance between us. Her hips bumped into the counter behind her as our skin met. Her lashes swept down, and she took a shuddering breath.

"Fuck me," I growled on the heels of a ragged breath.

"Please do."

I sensed she was trying to tease me, but her words came out entirely serious.

Clinging to what little control I had, I opened my eyes before stepping back slightly and looking down. Her breasts were plump, her nipples deep pink and drawn tight to pebbled peaks. Dipping my head, I brought my mouth to one, teasing lightly with my tongue before letting my mouth close over it and sucking it in. I savored her sharp cry as I teased her other nipple with my thumb and forefinger, pinching it gently.

Her palm curled around my shaft, stroking upward to draw a bead of pre-cum at the tip. I felt it rolling down along my length before her thumb swiped over the crown, smearing the moisture. I was already teetering on the edge of release.

I lifted my head, meeting her gaze, which was as needy and frantic as mine. I stepped back. In a rush, she shimmied out of her leggings as I shoved my jeans down just enough. I was about to lift her onto the counter before sanity reached me, for a moment breaking through the fog of fierce lust. I fumbled for my wallet in my back pocket, nearly dropping it before

I tossed it on the counter and slipped out the one and only condom I'd ever carried in there.

It's not like I was a busy guy, not lately. But old habits die hard. Years back, my mom had told me to always keep a condom in my wallet, so I did.

"Hurry," she urged as I smoothed it on.

A moment later, I lifted her onto the counter, reaching between her thighs to find her slippery wet. Glancing down, I watched as her thighs fell open, and I teased my fingers at her entrance. She was pink, glistening with her arousal. I felt those claws of need so sharply it almost hurt.

"Hurry," she demanded again.

I slid her hips to the edge of the counter. Our eyes locked together as I nudged forward, notching my cock at her entrance. I held still for a beat to ask, "Are you sure you want this?"

Her dark gaze held mine as she lifted her chin slightly. Her reply was almost a demand. "Yes. Now."

I rocked forward slightly, and she curled her legs around my hips. I filled her in one swift thrust. Her tight, clenching core rippled around me. I clung to the thinnest thread of control as I tried not to let my release take over instantly. My voice was slurred as I murmured, "Fuck."

"Please," she panted as she rolled her hips against mine.

Time felt suspended, both rushed and slowed. All I knew was the feel of her skin against mine, her breasts brushing my chest with every rock of my hips into hers, and the tight fusion of our joining. Every thrust went deeper. I could feel her tightening around me, her release on the edge. Gripping her hip with one hand, I reached between us, teasing my fingers over the swollen bud of her clit.

One of her hands was at the base of my spine, and I felt the press of her fingers into my corded muscles as she cried out sharply, her entire body trembling.

I finally let go, the release that had been threatening for too many minutes snapping through me. The force of it was like something breaking free inside as I gasped her name.

Sensation danced through my system like little sparks flickering. My heartbeat was still thundering, and I felt stripped raw, so awash in pleasure I almost couldn't think past it. My mind was hazed. My senses gradually settled, and like the aftermath of a storm, the air was clear and crisp. I cataloged the small sensations—the feel of Wes's palm curled over my hip, and his other one just on the inside of my thigh where I could feel the calloused surface of his fingertips. His muscled chest was a contrast to my soft curves. I savored the dusting of hair on his chest and how it slightly prickled against my skin. I could feel his heartbeat slowing along with mine.

I suddenly felt bashful, a surprising feeling. For me, sex was, well, just a thing you did. That was what hurt so badly about my friend because that was my first experience with really caring about someone. Until him, sex had been a practical exchange that hadn't lived up to my expectations. I shoved those thoughts away. I felt vulnerable here and didn't know how to defend myself against the urge to trust Wes.

Wes's hand slid off my thigh, curling around my waist and moving up my back in a comforting pass. His fingers teased in my hair, sifting through it.

"Tiffany," he murmured, his voice low and gravelly.

I took a breath, marshaling my nerves, and then lifted my head to find his eyes waiting for mine. When our gazes met, I felt a shock in my solar plexus. The electrifying sensation was as if he'd grabbed ahold of my heart.

We stared at each other quietly. It felt as if we were each taking a measure of the other. His words surprised me.

"I don't think that worked."

"What do you mean?"

His lips curled just barely at the corners, but it was enough to send my belly into a swoop.

"The whole getting it out of our system. Complete failure," he said, his tone wry.

He couldn't know it, but I needed that. A giggle slipped out. I wasn't the kind of woman who giggled. I was very practical.

"Definitely not," I agreed.

His hand slipped free of my hair in the back, and he lifted it, brushing a loose lock off my cheek as he dipped his head and dusted a kiss over my lips.

A moment later, we untangled ourselves. Wes was solicitous, helping me off the counter and handing me my clothes. He went into the bathroom to dispose of his condom. When he came back out, he was pulling his shirt on. I was ridiculously disappointed to see his muscled chest disappear behind the fabric of his T-shirt.

I had busied myself putting plates in the dishwasher and boxing up the pizza. He rested his hips against the counter as he looked over at me. "I'd like to stay," he said, his honesty surprising me.

I opened my mouth to say that he could, but he added, "But that might be confusing for Ross."

I took a quick breath, nodding in agreement. Because that was the truth, and it was sensible. We'd gone from kissing to something unexpected and surprisingly powerful.

"Right," I said, trying to sound practical and calm.

"How about we have brunch tomorrow?"

"Uh, okay."

He grinned as he looked over at me. "Did I surprise you?"

I shrugged, feeling bashful again. "I guess so."

"I could say it's because it's good for us to spend time together with Ross, which is true, but I also like spending time with you."

My heartbeat kicked up a notch and my belly swooped again. Wes was unexpected and too much of what I wanted.

I decided to be honest. "I like spending time with you too. Where should we meet?"

"Firehouse Café," he said as if there could be any other answer.

I grinned. "Perfect. What time?"

"Nine."

———

A little bit later, I lay in bed after Wes kissed me goodbye and nearly buckled my knees at the door. My skin felt oversensitive. My nerve endings were overwrought from Wes.

I stared at the ceiling, my eyes tracing the glow-in-the-dark star constellations someone else had left here before I moved into this apartment. My practical self was trying to be heard through the cacophony of need and my bruised heart wanting so much.

I fell asleep, telling myself not to be stupid and not to be foolish. But my sensible, guarded heart knew I was treading far past the line of foolishness.

"Hey, man," a voice said from behind me just as a hand clapped my shoulder.

Glancing back, I found Chase Mills, Tiffany's older brother, behind me in line with his fiancée, Hallie.

"Hey," I said, my mind immediately flashing to the feel of Tiffany's soft, warm, and bare-naked skin against me. I fiercely kicked those thoughts to the curb. I did *not* need to think about my friend's little sister right now. Fuck my life. What wasn't supposed to be complicated was becoming *far* more complicated than I'd anticipated.

I worked with Chase and liked the guy. He was solid, dependable, and just an all-around decent guy. He'd probably kick my fucking ass if he knew what I'd been doing with his sister last night.

I glanced at Hallie with a smile. Her soft brown hair fell in a swingy bob around her shoulders. She lifted her hand, pressing the center of her glasses up on her nose. "Hi, Wes. How are things?"

"Good," I replied. "How are you?" I could do this. I had good manners and could handle a basic conversation with them. Tiffany's brother *never* needed to know what happened.

Chase slid his arm around Hallie's shoulders. "Pretty good," she was saying. "The baby keeps us busy."

"I hear babies do that," I quipped.

She laughed. "They do. But I get to have coffee now that I've had the baby, so that's a win."

I chuckled. "I would miss coffee."

"You're family now," Hallie commented next.

"I am?"

Chase flashed an easy grin. "You and Tiffany are taking care of Ross. Family is what you make it."

Archer Cannon approached with his wife, Phoebe. He heard the tail end of Chase's comment and grinned. "It is." Archer glanced at me. "Did you know we were cousins?" He thumbed toward Chase.

"Uh, can't say I knew that," I replied.

Chase chuckled. "We are. It's a long story."

"You can explain over dinner," Hallie chimed in.

"Are we planning a dinner?" Phoebe asked. "We can host at our place."

The next thing I knew, I was invited to dinner with Chase, Hallie, Archer, and Phoebe. Just then, the bell chimed at the café, and Tiffany came walking in with Ross. The second my eyes collided with hers, I felt the force of our connection viscerally, a jolting vibration through my entire system.

Tiffany stopped beside Chase and Hallie. "Hey." Ross looked amongst the faces. He had already met Chase.

Chase was great, rounding to the other side of him and lifting his hand to give him a high five. "Hey, dude. How's Nilla?"

Ross smiled. "Good, I think."

Chase glanced toward me before his eyes bounced to Tiffany. "You should bring them out to our place. Nilla can meet Jasper."

"Who's Jasper?" Ross asked.

"My dog," Chase replied with a grin.

"You have a dog too?" Ross's eyes widened.

"I do."

Hallie smiled down at Ross. "He's technically Chase's dog, but I love him too."

"We're just planning a dinner party," Phoebe commented to Tiffany.

"We are? Tell me when, and I'll be there. Are we all having coffee together?" she asked.

Phoebe replied, "We're just getting some to go. Archer's parents are here, and his mom is at the house making omelets for breakfast before they fly back to Fireweed Harbor this afternoon."

"We're just picking up as well," Chase said.

"We're out of coffee at the house," Hallie chimed in. "I wasn't in charge of grocery shopping this week."

Tiffany's eyes glinted with mirth as she glanced at her brother. "I think you forgot the coffee."

He shrugged, looking sheepish. "I did."

I was relieved at the bustle of multiple people ordering. It was hard enough to keep my attention off Tiffany. I was also relieved that Ross had a running list of questions for Chase and me about video games. He even planned a time each week for us to play together.

Chase looked at me. "Dude, he's better than both of us. I'm going to have to brush up on my skills."

Ross thought that was hysterical.

Not much later, I was with Tiffany and Ross at a table. He wanted to play a game on my phone. After conferring with Tiffany via text even though we were sitting at the table together, I decided to let him. I would have to look into things about screen time for kids. I felt like I had literally been thrown into the deep end of parenting and was barely treading water. I figured I could keep Ross alive, but that might be it at this point.

"So how'd it go last night?" I asked after I'd handed my phone over to him.

Ross looked up. "Good. I like my room." He glanced back and forth between us, a small smile teasing at the corners of his lips when he added, "I think it's funny you want the room to match at your house."

I gestured toward Tiffany. "All credit to Tiff on that."

Something chased through his eyes, and I worried. He'd just lost both of his parents. Here he was with us, and it must've felt strange. Even though we knew his parents well, we didn't know him well. I remembered vaguely what it was like when I was his age. We must've seemed like complete strangers. I only hoped we could stumble our way through this, and it would be okay for him.

Tiffany chatted with a woman who paused by the table, and I took the moment to surreptitiously look at her. Her dark hair was pulled up this morning in an artful twist with a few locks dangling along the side of her neck and cheeks. I wanted to lean over and press my lips to the soft skin just behind her ear. I had cataloged so many tiny details about her last night, including that she shivered in my arms and goosebumps prickled across the surface of her skin when I'd kissed her right there.

The woman glanced at her watch. "I have to run. We're so glad Alice is here, and the vet clinic is back to full force." The woman's hand fell onto Tiffany's shoulder, and she squeezed lightly. "It's good to have you back in town. I know your father is thrilled."

They said their goodbyes, and Tiffany glanced at me. "Customer from the vet clinic," she explained. "She knows my dad somehow, and I'm not even sure how." She shrugged.

"Life in a small town," I offered.

She smiled over at me, and an unfamiliar sensation slipped through me with a sense of warmth spinning around my heart.

Ross clenched a fist and whispered, "Yes!"

"You over there kicking butt and taking names?" I teased.

His eyes lifted to mine, and he grinned as he nodded. "How long can I play?"

I glanced at Tiffany, unsure how to respond. She shrugged. "Carry on. I think Wes and I have to brush up on rules like this." She paused, her hesitation incremental, but I sensed when she made the decision to go ahead. "What were your parents' rules about phone games and video games? According to Wes and Chase, you're pretty good, so obviously, you got to play."

An odd expression crossed his face, perhaps sadness mixed with a hint of relief, maybe that someone mentioned his parents. I knew I was tiptoeing around that topic. The therapist had suggested we make sure not to avoid mentioning them because that might make him afraid to talk about them. She had gently pointed out that grief took its own course for everyone and explained that trying to pretend it didn't happen didn't help anyone.

Ross's small shoulders lifted as he took a breath. I noticed his fingers tighten incrementally along the edges of my phone as he looked back and forth between us. "I could play. Dad played video games."

"He sure did," I interjected. "He and I used to play online at the same time sometimes."

Ross looked at me, his eyes widening and a smile stretching across his face. "That's cool."

I dipped my chin in acknowledgment. "Your dad was a cool guy."

Ross's gaze sobered again as he offered, "As long as I did my homework and chores, I could have an hour and a half of either TV or video games." He looked around the café. "If we were out and about like this, Dad would let me play on his phone."

I studied my friend's son and knew he was being honest. My heart twisted sharply.

"I think those rules are absolutely fair," Tiffany said with an enthusiastic nod.

"But you haven't given me any chores," Ross replied.

"We haven't, but we'll figure that one out," she replied.

Janet arrived with our coffee and a caramel hot chocolate for Ross. She smiled, adding, "Just shout if you need something else. Your food's going to be about twenty minutes." She gave us an apologetic smile and gestured with her hand around the café, which was packed. All the tables were full, and there was still a line at the register.

"It's no problem," Tiffany replied. She took a quick sip of her coffee, letting out a satisfied sigh. "The coffee is delicious. Thank you."

Janet rushed off. When Ross looked down at his game, I glanced at Tiffany, and she shrugged. Even though I was really getting to know her all over again, I knew she was referencing that she hoped we handled that conversation well.

I nodded. Without thinking, I reached over and

slid my palm on top of her thigh. When I saw her eyes widen slightly and a flush crest on her cheeks, I almost pulled my hand away. But I didn't want to. She surprised me by placing her hand over mine, then turning it over and interlacing our fingers.

My heart tumbled in my chest, and I squeezed lightly, feeling a subtle sense of joy bloom inside my chest. My life had been busy this past year with moving back to Willow Brook and my mom needing extra help here and there, so I hadn't thought much about romance. I'd had one sort of serious relationship in college. Nothing awful happened. We graduated and went our separate ways.

Between hotshot firefighting and helping cover the rescue program for my mom, I was insanely busy. Toss in the fact that I was unexpectedly sharing guardianship for one of my best friend's sons, and my entire life felt topsy-turvy.

When I looked at Tiffany, she bit her lip before glancing away and lifting her coffee cup to take another swallow. I shifted my hand, caressing along the side of her wrist with my thumb. When her lashes lifted and the blue of her eyes darkened slightly as she looked over at me, I had to swallow and take a quick breath, tearing my gaze away.

Ross's thumbs moved furiously on the phone screen. He was deep in concentration. When our food arrived, I reluctantly released Tiffany's hand.

I was typing furiously, entering the information a distraught owner was sharing on the phone. "Just come on in," I said when she paused. "Alice has time this afternoon to see him."

"Oh, thank God!" Beth, the owner, said. "I'll be there as soon as I can. I should be able to make it in about thirty minutes."

After I ended that call, my phone quacked like a duck. That was my reminder for our lunch break. I stood quickly from the desk, hurrying to the door and turning the sign to *Closed for Lunch*.

Alice was getting busy enough that she wanted to be able to fit in emergencies when she could. We needed to hire a vet tech ASAP.

I strode to the back, peering into the area where Alice did her charting. Her last morning appointment had left only moments ago. She glanced up, blowing a puff of air from her lip and effectively getting a lock of hair tangled on the corner of her glasses.

I grinned. "Slick."

She rolled her eyes. "Is it official lunchtime?"

"Yes, ma'am. Let's hustle. I already locked the door, but you have an emergency coming in."

"Oh no! what happened?" Alice asked as she stood from where she'd been seated on a stool by a table, following me across the hallway into the break room.

"It sounds to me like the dog got into something. But the dog mama is distraught because her dog has vomited and had diarrhea. Apparently, the diarrhea is really runny and stinky."

I shook my head a little. I'd never realized how much I would discuss poop working at a vet clinic.

Alice snorted as she crossed over to the coffee pot, quickly filling a mug for herself and tossing over her shoulder, "Do you want some?"

"Yes, please." I opened the refrigerator, adding, "I made pasta salad for us."

We'd settled into a habit of taking turns making lunch for each other. This was turning out to be the best job I'd ever had. My remaining challenge was wearing Alice down until she acknowledged she needed to hire a vet tech. She was kind of nervous about it, thinking she was going to take on too much salary in the budget.

"Anything else I need to know about the dog coming in?" she asked as we sat down together.

She passed over a mug of coffee for me, and I handed her the plastic container of pasta salad prepared for her. I opened my own and handed over a fork.

"Nope," I replied. "She'll be here in a half hour, which gives us time to eat. Her dog's name is Lassie. She's a mutt and the best dog in the world."

Alice grinned just as we heard Honey's distinctive three-legged gait trotting down the hallway. Honey entered the room, pausing to get pets from both of us before she curled up on her dog bed in the corner.

Just then, my cell phone vibrated, and I spun it around on the table. I quickly glanced at the screen to see an automated text from the doctor's office in Anchorage. It was my test results, but I didn't want to look at them now.

Alice was chewing, but her eyes were on me as soon as my gaze lifted. "What?" I asked.

"You look a little worried."

"I'm not worried," I lied, ignoring the reflexive twist of anxiety that rose whenever I had anything to do with doctors lately. A medical scare would do that to you, even if it turned out okay.

Her brows arched toward her hairline, her lips pursing as she finished chewing. She took another quick bite of pasta salad, offering, "This is yummy."

"It's one of my staples," I said, relieved that she was letting the topic drop.

It was penne pasta with a dash of olive oil, red pepper flakes, feta cheese, sliced black olives, and red peppers with shredded chicken added to it for protein.

"I need the recipe," she replied.

"I'll write it down. I promise it's easy."

She nodded. "For someone whose job it is to ask all kinds of people personal questions, you sure keep a lot to yourself."

"I should've known you weren't letting that topic drop," I muttered, stabbing a piece of pasta with my fork and chewing it quickly.

"You look worried, and I care about you. What the hell is up with that text message?"

"Just test results from my doctor."

"Oh, the doctor you went to see in Anchorage that you also didn't mention?"

"Are you snooping?" I was genuinely affronted.

She rolled her eyes. "No, but you must've given the office number as backup, and they left a message reminding you of your appointment last week. I asked if you knew you had a doctor's appointment, remember?"

I lightly smacked my forehead with the heel of my hand. "That's right. Fine. I had to go see a neurology specialist in Anchorage."

"Neurologist? What aren't you telling me?" Alice rested her fork against the edge of the container. She took a gulp of coffee, her eyes pinned to mine.

"Fine," I grumbled. "I'll just tell you so you know I'm fine. They had me schedule a follow-up a year after my surgery for the nerve sheath tumor last year. I was supposed to follow up with a neurologist here to make sure I didn't have any lingering symptoms and the growth hasn't returned. I'm good to go. I had an excellent surgeon in Seattle, and they didn't even damage any of the nerves taking it out."

"I've heard nerve sheath tumors can be seriously painful," Alice said. She took a bite of her pasta, chewing rapidly as if she were angry with it.

"What the hell did the pasta do to you?" I teased.

She finished chewing and pointed her fork at me. "Nothing. I was just a little stressed out to learn this. I'm glad you're still fine, and I appreciate you telling me. Why all the secrecy?"

I shrugged. "I don't know. I guess I didn't want to freak anybody out until I knew for sure I was still fine."

"Do your dad and Chase know what happened?" I hesitated just long enough that Alice narrowed her eyes. "You didn't tell them?"

"No." I grimaced. "Now, it's this thing that's not a

thing. I don't want to make it a big deal when everything is fine."

"You're fucked up," my friend announced.

"Everybody's fucked up."

She gestured to my phone. "So you're all good?"

"Well, I was going to check the results right now," I muttered. "The doctor texted earlier and said everything looked good, but they'd send the results."

"Open your fucking results," Alice ordered.

I groaned, setting my fork down and lifting my phone. She was not going to let me blow this off.

After I logged into the online portal, she held her hand out. "Let me see."

"This is private information," I hedged even though I didn't care if she saw it.

"You said everything was fine, and you're my friend. Either read them to me or show me."

I simply handed my phone over to her. Her eyes skimmed the screen. "No more pain?" she asked.

I shook my head. "None. There was a little numbness right around the area afterward. They said that might remain because they had to remove it directly off the nerve sheath, but the numbness went away. I'm not having the breathtaking pain anymore."

"I'm giving you homework," she announced as she handed my phone back.

"Excuse me?"

Alice nodded, finishing the bite she'd just taken. "You need to tell your father and Chase what happened. I don't care if you don't want to tell them about your dumb ex who turned out to be an idiot and an asshole, but you had surgery on your back, and you didn't tell anybody in your family about it. I get wanting to keep things private and not freak people out, but I'd willingly give up a limb if I had parents to worry about telling these kinds of things to."

"Okay," I said, feeling chagrined since her parents had died, and I knew she missed them. She had a point. "I probably should've told them sooner. I kind of panicked when I started having pain. When they ordered the MRI and found a growth, I panicked even more, and it just mushroomed into this thing I didn't want anybody to worry about. I'll tell them." I took a swallow of coffee as she gave a satisfied nod. "Speaking of Chase, he and Hallie and Archer and Phoebe want us to have a dinner get-together with Wes and me and to bring Ross."

"Like a couples thing?" Alice asked, a slight glint in her eyes.

"Wes and I are *not* a couple," I ground out.

My friend let out a knowing chuckle. "If you say so."

Phoebe had just opened the door to the house and was saying hello when a boy came running down the hallway, letting out what could only be a whoop and spinning a small lasso in the air. "I didn't know you had a son," I commented as Archer approached.

He chuckled. "We don't. This is our neighbor's son. They're out of town for the weekend."

"Ah, that makes sense. I know I haven't been back in town that long, but I thought I would've known if you had kids since Phoebe and I see each other at the station on the regular."

Phoebe was one of several female firefighters at the station and happened to be on my crew. As she closed the door behind me, I glanced around the space, my eyes returning to Archer. "It looks the same but different."

This was Archer's childhood home. We had been friends in elementary school before he moved away in middle school. You wouldn't know it, but Archer's family was wealthy—like ridiculously wealthy. The Cannon family owned Fireweed Industries, which had started as a small winery and brewery in Fireweed Harbor. When they had some success a few decades earlier, they'd bought up properties and expanded into ventures all over Alaska and then all over the world. His parents had owned and run a mine near Willow Brook when he was younger before they shut it down. He had returned recently and renovated the entire business into a renewable energy company.

Archer winked as he looked around. "It does look the same but different. The bones of the house are good. We had Amelia and Lucy help us renovate it."

"Come on in." Phoebe gestured for me to follow her.

We crossed through an entryway into the main living room. It was an open-concept home with a tall, angled ceiling and a wall of windows, offering a stunning view out over a field with the mountains and a glacier in the distance, complete with a wide stream crossing through the side of the field. From the living room, there was an arched opening into the kitchen and a hallway that led to bedrooms and an upper floor.

"Over here." Phoebe pointed at a comfortable-looking sofa. Just beyond that was a buffet selection of food on a sideboard.

"Are you cooking?" I glanced at Archer.

He shook his head with a grin. "I can handle the basics. When we decided we were doing this, I ordered some platters from Wildlands," he explained, referencing a favorite local restaurant.

Phoebe interjected, "We were both busy today, so this seemed easier. Where is Ross?" The boy who I'd yet to meet came running back down the hallway.

"We were hoping Tommy would have someone to hang out with tonight," Archer added. "They're about the same age, I think. How old is Ross?"

"Eight," I replied.

"Oh, they're the same age. Perfect," Phoebe said.

"Tiffany's bringing him," I supplied.

"Do you want some hors d'oeuvres?" Phoebe gestured to the platters of appetizers on the sideboard. "We were going to get the buffalo wings, but I thought the nuggets were less messy," she explained as I perused the food selection.

The assortment included a platter of chicken nuggets with various sauces, another platter of halibut bites and sliders, and a giant tray of nachos. Archer handed me a plate, and we both grabbed a few things to eat. As we walked over to the large sectional sofa, I asked, "And who else is going to be here tonight?"

"Chase and Hallie. Of course, you and Tiffany and Ross. Russell and Paisley said they'd be by. We invited Graham and Madison, but Graham's daughter has an overnight with a friend, and he point blank told me they were taking the night for themselves." Archer rolled his eyes at that.

"I think that's how it goes when you have a kid full-time," I offered dryly.

We sat down as Phoebe brought over glasses of water, asking if I wanted a beer.

"I'll take one. I'm driving so no more than that. What do you have?"

"Something from Diamond Creek Brewery." She brought out a variety six-pack.

"This place is good," I commented as I made my selection.

"Have you heard?" Phoebe asked as she sat down. "There's a brewery coming to town."

"Seriously?" I asked before taking a bite of one of the chicken nuggets. A burst of honey with a spicy hint exploded in my mouth.

Phoebe nodded. "Seriously. I'm not sure who it is, but my mom's heard about it. They've applied for the business license."

"That'll be nice. I hope it's good."

Just then, the doorbell chimed. Phoebe started to get up, but Archer shook his head, setting his plate on the large square coffee table. "I've got it."

As he stood and crossed the living room to answer the door, Phoebe glanced at me. "How's it going with Ross?"

I thought for a moment as I finished chewing another bite. "Good, I think. I think all of us, myself and Tiffany included, are still adjusting. I'm not sure what they were thinking. Neither one of us has ever been a parent."

"But they were your best friends, right?"

She popped a sweet potato fry in her mouth as I replied, "George was my best friend in college. Turns out, Sarah and Tiffany became close when Sarah lived in Willow Brook during high school, and then they went to college together. Sarah transferred to one of those accelerated legal programs, and she and George met after that. They had Ross right after they graduated. Back when he was born, George asked me to be Ross's godfather. It's not like I didn't take it seriously, but I just never expected..." I lifted a hand, palm up, before letting it fall.

Phoebe nodded in agreement. "I get it. If a close friend of mine asked me to be a guardian if something happened, I'd say yes, but I would assume nothing would ever happen."

"The attorney said they knew I wouldn't be able to be a full-time parent because of my schedule. It's just..." I shook my head slowly. "I don't know anything about this kind of grief. I hope Ross will be okay."

Archer was saying something at the door, and I heard Tiffany's voice. Before I even looked in her direction, my pulse skyrocketed. I glanced over quickly before bringing my attention back to Phoebe. "All in all, I feel like he's still almost in shock. He's a good kid."

My eyes were instantly drawn back in the direction of Tiffany as Archer was closing the door. Ross was at her side. My heart clenched for a beat. I could see a hint of uncertainty about him.

"You and Tiffany are both good people. This is a challenge for a gazillion obvious reasons," Phoebe said as I glanced back at her. "But he's in good hands."

"I hope so," I said.

Just then, Tommy came running down the stairs, skidding to a stop beside Ross. Ross looked a little surprised.

"Hi!" Tommy said

Ross blinked and then smiled slightly. "Hi."

"Want to play video games?" Tommy asked.

"Do I get to play?" Archer teased.

Ross and Tommy peered up at him, with Ross replying, "Sure."

Archer winked, clapping him lightly on the shoulder. "No need. If it's okay with Tiffany and"—he glanced over at me—"Wes, I'll walk you guys down to the game room. Want to check it out?"

I set my plate down on the coffee table, standing as I replied, "Of course. Ross is kicking my butt at games on the regular."

Archer introduced himself as they began walking down the hallway. Tommy immediately interjected to ask Ross about his favorite games. I glanced at Archer, saying under my breath, "Thank you."

A few minutes later, they were situated in what was

apparently Archer's home office. Aside from the desk, there was a small couch with a TV and a video console in the corner. "All right, guys. Play nice. I'll check on you in a few minutes," Archer said.

I glanced down at Ross. "Are you hungry? I can bring you a plate."

He was already lifting the gaming controller as he looked up at me, nodding. "Nothing messy, or I'll get the controller dirty."

I chuckled. "Got it. I'll bring something in a few minutes."

When I returned to the living room, Tiffany was seated with a plate just beside where I'd been sitting. Considering that my plate was right there on the coffee table, it only made sense that I should sit beside her. Even though I knew it would send my hormones into overdrive, I did. I felt caught between two urges: the urge to keep my distance—and, therefore, my sanity—and the urge to be close. My response to her was so powerful the force of it was hard to override.

"Hi," she said when I sat beside her and picked up my plate.

The second our gazes collided, a pink flush tinged her cheeks. I willed myself not to get aroused.

"Hi," I said simply before popping a spicy buffalo nugget in my mouth, hoping the food would keep my body's reaction under a bare minimum of control.

I thought the least I could do was not behave like a randy adolescent boy with an audience of friends.

The doorbell chimed just as Archer happened to be walking back into the room from the kitchen. He stopped and opened it. Chase and Hallie had arrived.

Fuck my life. Having Tiffany's brother here as part of the audience only weakened my already slipping control.

Somehow, I managed to be polite. The conversation carried on. I left the room after finishing my plate to bring one to Ross and deliver one Phoebe had made for Tommy. I thought I was pulling this thing off. I could be around Tiffany without wanting to tear her clothes off. It involved studiously avoiding looking directly at her and making sure not to touch her. My fingertips itched to touch her since she was seated beside me, but I had it under control.

Totally. It was all fine and well.

I even planned a dipnetting trip with Chase, Russell, and Archer this summer. We were joking about how it was easier to go as a group so we could help each other carry our coolers. Dipnetting in the summers in Alaska was insanely fun. It was a ton of work, but it usually resulted in a chest freezer full of fresh salmon.

Russell and I also planned a day of backcountry skiing, which I hadn't had a chance to do since I got home. Chase and Hallie offered to babysit if we needed it.

At some point, Tiffany went to check on Ross, and I needed to go to the bathroom. Phoebe directed me to the one off a small alcove that led from the kitchen into the garage. I finished washing my hands and stepped out to find Tiffany waiting.

Chapter Twenty-One

WES

Tiffany's eyes widened when she saw me. "Oh," she said, her voice coming out low and husky.

One single word out of her mouth, and my body felt singed from the heat coursing through it. The arousal I'd been trying to keep at bay all evening swelled.

We stared at each other in the small space. We were protected from view, and no one was in the kitchen. All of the voices were a distant murmur.

"Ross seems to be making a friend," I observed.

Tiffany nodded, staying right where she was with her back against the wall. I wasn't thinking when I stepped closer. "How are you?" I asked, resting a hand on the wall beside her.

Her eyes met mine, and the sound of her breath drawing in sharply was like a little bolt of lightning, electrifying the air around us.

"Okay," she whispered.

We stared at each other as my heart thudded hard and fast against my rib cage. "I need to kiss you," I murmured.

I stepped closer yet again. Our bodies were flush now, and I could feel her nipples, tight little peaks, pressing through the fabric of her shirt and mine. My cock throbbed. I knew she felt my arousal, nestled in the cradle of her hips. She shifted slightly, just enough that her hips rocked against me.

I let out a low growl before dipping my head and claiming her mouth in a kiss. For a moment, my mind went blank when her tongue glided against mine. She made this little sound in her throat. I rocked into her, and her hips rolled to meet my motion. Abruptly, I remembered where we were. As if we were entirely in tune, we broke apart at the same time, staring at each other.

Her breath came in little pants. I leaned my head back, scrambling for control. When my gaze met hers again, she bit her lip. It was all I could do not to start kissing her again.

"I want you," I said flatly.

She let out a startled, almost disbelieving laugh. "Wes, this is crazy."

"I know." I rocked against her again, and she released a little moan. "Fuck," I muttered.

"We have to get it together," she said quickly.

I took another deep breath, marshaling my discipline and stepping back reluctantly.

Somehow, I got the need raging inside me under control and managed, or at least I thought I did, to return to the living room and socialize like a normal human being. I was profoundly relieved the evening was winding down because looking Chase in the eyes was challenging.

"Is that okay with you?" Tiffany's question broke through my fuzzy thoughts.

I'd been so damn busy trying not to look at her

that I'd lost the thread of the conversation. "Excuse me, I zoned out. Is what okay?"

When I glanced up, my gaze passed briefly by Hallie's. There was a mischievous, knowing glint in her eyes. I forced myself to look at Tiffany.

"Tommy asked if Ross could spend the night," she explained.

"Tomorrow," Phoebe chimed in. "He can stay here."

"They can have my office for the whole night," Archer said with a dry chuckle.

"If it's okay with you all, it's definitely okay with me." I glanced at Ross. "What about you?" He nodded enthusiastically. "Sounds like a plan. What time should I bring him over?" I looked over toward Archer and Phoebe.

"Let's say five," Phoebe said. "Archer was already planning a pizza night."

"I love any excuse for pizza," Archer said with a wink. "And we were planning to do a fire outside with marshmallows, s'mores, the whole deal. That'll be dessert. If I can break these guys away from video games, that is."

"I've never had a campfire," Ross piped up.

"You're in for a treat," Tiffany offered with a warm smile. "They're the best in the winter."

Fuck me. I could not even look at her, not if I wanted to hold my need at bay.

Chapter Twenty-Two

TIFFANY

It was late, and I was restless. I'd never been a great sleeper, even when I was younger. Maybe it was the wondering about how things were with my mom or the occasional fraught arguments she would start with my dad. It was almost as if it angered her that he was a steady, stable presence in our lives and hers. Whenever it came to my mother when I was a little girl, a churning sense of uncertainty mingled with a needy wish for her to pay more attention to me and not to view me as an inconvenience, for her to want me, to love me.

As an adult, I could see that she did the best she could, which was not very good at all. Her own sense of need felt yawning sometimes, as if she couldn't get enough of what she hoped from the world and those around her. I had a distant recollection of my grandparents, her parents. They'd not been very warm or very stable and were mostly distant, like her. I recalled they both died sometime during elementary school, but the details were thin.

As I'd gotten a better sense of what my father had

given me and my brother, I understood that he gave us the very quality she simply didn't have—we mattered because of us, not because of what he needed from us. His steady love felt like a soft ray of sunshine, casting warmth and light.

Yet I still couldn't believe love was worth it. Not even trying was the safe, smart option.

"Ugh," I muttered to myself, rolling onto my stomach and groaning into my pillow.

My insides were churning. This whole thing with Wes was muddling my emotions. I wished, desperately, that I didn't want him so much. Our kiss tonight had felt like the equivalent of flooring the gas pedal on the need racing through me. I couldn't find the brakes to slow it down.

Even now, my arousal was still present, dancing like hot sparks through my veins.

I took a breath, rolling onto my back and ordering myself to stop thinking so much about Wes. My body was doing the opposite of everything I demanded. The second I tried to kick him out of my thoughts, he came back with insistence. I could remember the feel of his hands on my skin, his lips molding over mine, and the way he felt inside me.

My phone vibrated on my nightstand. Without touching my phone or even looking at the screen, I knew it was Wes. I told myself not to look, but I couldn't help it. Like everything with him, my body had a mind of its own, driven by a force beyond my control.

Reaching over, I snagged the phone. The text banner displayed his name.

Wes: *Are you awake?*

My face felt hot. My body was so sensitive, so attuned to him that the mere fact he texted me from miles away had my skin feeling hypersensitive. My nipples tightened, and I could feel the fabric of my tank top lightly abrading them. I was smiling as I typed out my reply.

Me: *Yes.*

The dots indicating that he was typing appeared almost instantly, and I could feel the drum roll of my heartbeat pounding through my body as I waited. Butterflies twirled in my belly, sending tingles scattering through my system. My legs shifted restlessly.

Wes: *I was thinking you could come over tomorrow night. I'll make you dinner.*

I bit my lip, smiling to myself.

Me: *Is this a date?*

My pussy clenched, and I became acutely aware of the arousal slick between my thighs.

Wes: *Yes. I just want to see you.*

My heart pounded faster.

Me: *Well, I guess it's good I want to see you too.*

Wes: *Sweetheart, I want more than to see you.*

I stared at the screen, trying to calm down. Before I could talk myself out of it, I swiped his contact to call him.

He answered immediately. "Tiffany."

"Hey," I whispered huskily.

"What are you doing?" he asked, the sound of his voice low and gravelly, sliding over my nerve endings like warm honey.

"Lying in bed, not falling asleep." He was quiet for a moment. "You're supposed to tell me this is stupid," I added.

"What if I don't care if it's stupid?"

"Wes," I whispered, his name almost a plea.

"Either I come all over my hand by myself or with you," he said, his words shocking and blunt.

My body reacted with my pussy clenching. Without thinking, my free hand slid over my belly, dipping past the thin elastic of my practical cotton panties. My fingers dipped down into my folds. They were slippery wet, and my clit was a swollen bud. I couldn't hold back the little whimper that escaped.

"Tell me how wet you are."

His low command elicited an immediate response with my hips bucking. "Wes," I pleaded.

"How close are you?" he asked

I couldn't help myself. My fingers swirled around my clit, sliding back and forth. My release was waiting, a sharp piercing need.

"Almost there," I choked out.

My hips were rocking of their own accord, and oh, how I wanted him! Right here. With me. Filling me.

"Come with me." His voice was raw. "Now," he growled.

My body instantly followed his command. My release sizzled through me, everything going taut before breaking loose. Deep tremors raced through my body, the pleasure so fierce that everything was a haze in my thoughts as I gasped, crying his name.

The ripples slowed, the pleasure rolling through me in waves as I gradually caught my breath. I could hear the ragged sound of his breathing through the phone line as I slowly drew my fingers away, thinking I had never done this with anyone. In a way, it felt more intimate than being with him skin to skin. Because I was letting him bear witness to my need taking over.

"Do you think you'll fall asleep now?" he asked, his tone teasing. Yet I sensed he was also quite serious.

"Yes," I said with a low laugh.

"I will too. Sweet dreams, Tiffany."

"Wait."

"Yeah?"

"What time should I come over tomorrow?"

"Let's say five-thirty. I'm dropping Ross off at five at Phoebe and Archer's place. Any requests for dinner?"

"Surprise me."

Chapter Twenty-Three

TIFFANY

Hands on my hips, I watched as my father finished a shelf he was building in the garage at his house. He lightly tapped the top shelf down with a mallet on one side, saying, "There."

It was a simple yet elegant three-level shelf made of wood my father had planed himself.

"What's that for?"

"Ross. It's a shelf for his video games. See." He gestured. "The top shelf is for the console and then room for his games. I know he plays online, which I don't even understand." My father rolled his eyes. "But he said he has some games too. I'll make two shelves for him, one for your place and one for Wes's."

My heart squeezed as I looked at my father. He straightened and set the mallet on his workbench. I felt as if a string tugged on my heart, reminding me of how fiercely I loved my father. He had always worked to be a mainstay in my life, a source of stability while I had scrambled internally over the fractured relationship with my mother.

In the aftermath of our mother passing, learning about the two flings my mother had, strangely, didn't make things worse, at least not as to how I felt about her. It did tangle into the knot of mistrust I had about relationships. You could be a good person and still have someone treat you badly

"I love it, Dad," I said when I realized he was waiting for me to say something. "Ross will love it."

Just then, the sound of tires on gravel reached us. Glancing out the side door of the garage, I saw my brother's truck. "Oh, Chase is here."

My father nodded when my gaze swung back to him. "Yeah, he's dropping off some tools he borrowed." He turned and started tidying the shelf just beside his workbench. He was a man who kept things organized.

As Chase entered the garage, my father commented, "I'd love for you and Wes to come over for dinner with Ross. I may not play video games, but I still want to get to know him."

Chase grinned. "Ross kicks ass at video games, but Wes says he likes doing stuff outside. Maybe you could take him on one of your trips."

Our father had been a wilderness guide for years. He still did it but not as often as he used to. He was well known in the area and tended to be recommended to more experienced groups because he knew all the best places and was highly skilled as well as safe.

"That's a great idea. I've got a winter hike scheduled soon, just a day one. I'll see if he'd like to go."

"Sounds like a plan," Chase replied. His eyes shifted to me. "Tiffany could go with you."

"I don't like being cold," I said flatly. While I was an Alaskan girl, born and bred, I didn't like being cold.

I loved the outdoors, but when it came to winter, I liked looking at the snow and then hanging out in front of a warm fire.

Chase chuckled. "I know." He held up one of my father's familiar tool bags, saying, "Here you go."

"Thanks," my dad said lightly as he turned and crossed over to lift it from Chase's hand.

"What were you doing? It's not like you have any shortage of tools," I commented.

"I do have plenty of tools, but I don't have a hard-wood floor nailer."

"How are things going at the house?" I asked.

"Almost done," Chase said with a nod.

"Just in time for the baby," my father observed.

"I still can't believe you're a father!" I impulsively stepped to my brother and threw my arms around his waist to give him a quick hug. Chase returned my hug before stepping back with a grin.

"Here and there, I still can't believe it. Dad's got a bonus grandkid now."

Our father winked. "And I love it."

That sense of uncertainty unspooled inside me. I hadn't fully adjusted to the reality that Sarah had passed away. It was still startling the way it played out. I couldn't help but wonder why Sarah and George wanted Wes and me to share guardianship.

"Speaking of, what's up with you and Wes?" Chase asked.

I glanced at my brother, my eyes narrowing as I cast him a glare.

Our father looked back and forth between us. "What don't I know?"

"Nothing," I said too quickly.

My dad chuckled as he finished putting away the

last of his tools. "I need some coffee. I'm going to the kitchen to make it." He met my eyes. "Are you hanging out?"

"I need to run. I have a few errands to take care of."

My dad crossed over, dusting a kiss on my cheek and squeezing my shoulder lightly. "Give me a call. Maybe I'll text you the time for my winter day hike next weekend. If it works out for Ross, I'd love for him to come. Perhaps Wes could come with him if you don't want to."

With that, my father disappeared through the doorway that led from the garage into the kitchen, and I looked over at Chase. "What the hell?"

His brows hitched up as he gave me a knowing look. "You and Wes have something going on. I'm not blind. Everybody noticed. When I asked Hallie about it, she wouldn't say a word, which told me everything I needed to know."

I groaned. "Nothing is going on."

My brother studied me for a moment before his gaze softened. "You know, we both have our share of baggage from Mom. I'm living proof that it's worth letting go of that weight."

My throat felt tight, and tears stung my eyes. I experienced a familiar mix of annoyance and an old, achy pain in my heart. I wasn't about to fall apart in front of Chase, so I closed my eyes and took a deep breath, scrambling for some composure before I opened them again.

"I know," I said, striving to sound casual. "There's nothing to worry about with Wes and me. No matter what you think."

I was lying, but I wasn't ready to talk about it, not

with Chase, not when I already knew I was being foolish and reckless.

His eyes searched mine before he shrugged. "I'm here if you need me. He's an old friend, and I work with him, but if he hurts you, I'll kick his fucking ass."

And on *that* annoying note, I left.

Chapter Twenty-Four

WES

After taking a shower, I walked out of the bathroom and glanced around my bedroom. My mother had helped me furnish this house before I moved in. It had simple modern furniture with clean lines. The bed was piled high with pillows and a lightweight down quilt. I tried to imagine the space through Tiffany's eyes. Even though I lived as a bachelor, at least my place looked comfortable and clean.

I snorted to myself. I didn't usually worry about what a woman might think of where I lived. I could honestly say I'd never even considered it. Before moving back to Willow Brook, I'd mostly lived in apartments. As a hotshot firefighter, my life was nomadic because I moved where the season took me. When I decided to come back home to help my mom, one benefit was that the hotshot crews here had a home base. Alaska was big geographically with an unfortunate number of wildfires, but that meant there were year-round crews.

I shook my head, adjusting the towel where I'd wrapped it around my waist, and crossed over to open my dresser. I pulled out a pair of jeans and a Henley shirt, basically a uniform for me in the colder weather. A few minutes later, I was dressed and scrubbing a towel through my hair.

I walked into the living room area to find Nilla sitting by the door. Her tail thumped on the floor, and I chuckled. She'd quickly learned that if she wanted to go out, all she needed to do was sit by the door. I crossed over, saying, "Good girl," as I stroked her on the head. Opening the door, I let her out into the yard.

I watched from the windows as she trotted to the side by the trees where she had determined she should go to the bathroom. She did her business and frolicked in the snow for a few minutes before returning to the door and letting out a soft bark.

After I let her back in, I fed her before opening the refrigerator and pulling out the ingredients for dinner. Tiffany had said she would eat anything, so I'd decided to make a marinated salmon. My mom had given me some of her flash-frozen salmon from dipnetting last year. I was looking forward to that come summer. Ross would have a blast dipnetting. Dipnetting involved Alaskan resident-only fishing times where you could catch fresh wild salmon in nets as they swam upriver to spawn. Alaskans traveled in droves to the areas approved and stocked up on salmon for the winter.

Phoebe had texted she could pick Ross up because she was on her way into town for a grocery run and had Ross's new friend with her. Although I had adjusted to my new circumstances of sharing guardianship of a child, the whole thing was still strange. The attorney sent over the finalized guardianship paperwork with a note clarifying that if either of us wanted to complete adoption paperwork, she would be happy to do that at any point. I couldn't even wrap my brain around the idea that I felt like an instant parent.

After Nilla finished eating, she returned to the living room and leaped onto the back of the sofa. That was her favorite place when it was light out. Once darkness fell, she liked to sit in front of the wood stove. If there wasn't a fire, she would look at me expectantly until I started one.

I added a little extra marinade to the salmon and put the baking pan in the oven. After that, I adjusted the heat under some marinated vegetables I was searing in a pan. Nilla trotted back into the kitchen and nudged me with her nose. When I glanced down, she looked toward the woodstove. With a chuckle, I walked into the living room and gathered a few pieces of wood from the small rack beside it.

"I know what you want," I teased as her tail started wagging madly. Within minutes, I'd started a fire, and she happily sat down on the dog bed nearby, watching the flames through the glass door.

My phone vibrated on the kitchen counter as I returned. I glanced down to see a text from Tiffany. *On the way, be there in a few minutes.*

My heart started pounding a little faster as anticipation sizzled like fire in my veins. *It's just a text. It's just dinner.*

Who are you kidding? my skeptical voice volleyed back swiftly. *You've got it bad for Tiffany.*

It wasn't that I was opposed to relationships. I'd had a serious girlfriend in college. We'd simply broken up because life took us in different directions. We'd parted on good terms. After I became a hotshot firefighter, I was busy, traveling a lot. The job didn't lend itself to relationships.

I hadn't dated at all since I moved to Willow Brook. Not because I was avoiding it, but just because I was busy and honestly hadn't met anybody who sparked anything for me.

What I had felt for Tiffany was *so* much more than a spark. It was a fucking bonfire.

I forced my thoughts away from her and turned to check on the vegetables. It was only a few minutes before Nilla heard Tiffany's tires on the driveway. She got up and trotted over to the door, letting out a soft, expectant whine.

A moment later, Tiffany's headlights arced through the front window. That anticipation burned even hotter. I had her all to myself for the whole night.

She knocked just as my hand closed over the doorknob. I told myself to get a fucking grip. A blast of cold air came through when I opened it. She stood there in a small circle of light cast from the porch light. Her dark hair fell in a tousle around her shoulders, and her cheeks were pink. I wanted to kiss her instantly.

She smiled at me, blinking. "Hey," she said simply.

"Hey," I returned.

Nilla circled around her legs, snapping through my distraction as I realized I was standing there while Tiffany waited in the cold, and icy air blew into the house.

"Come in." I gestured her in as I opened the door wider.

Tiffany walked through, greeting Nilla as she danced around her legs in a happy circle. She smiled up at me, commenting, "She's really settling in."

I grinned down at Nilla. Tiffany shrugged out of her coat, hanging it on the row of hooks by the door and kicking off her boots. "It's supposed to snow tonight," she said as she turned away from the door.

"It's winter in Alaska."

She grinned just as the oven timer beeped.

"Follow me," I commented as I walked toward the kitchen.

"Can I help with anything?" she asked as I opened the oven and pulled out the baking pan.

"Everything's almost ready. I just need to put this under the broiler for a few minutes after I drain the marinade. Have a seat," I added, nudging my chin toward the kitchen table when I glanced over my shoulder.

Tiffany sat at the table, watching as I transferred the four salmon fillets from the marinade-filled pan to a baking sheet.

"What's in the marinade?" she asked.

"Balsamic vinegar, maple syrup, and pepper. My mom swears by it. Putting it under the broiler for a few minutes will caramelize the glaze," I explained.

"Oooh! You're an official cook."

I shrugged. "I don't know if anything about my cooking is official, but I enjoy it. My mom's a good cook and taught me while I was growing up. She said she refused to raise a son who didn't know his way around the kitchen."

"My dad's a pretty good cook and taught Chase too. And me," she added with a laugh. "I would call myself a serviceable cook. Nothing amazing.

"Is your dad around?" she asked, her tone uncertain.

"My parents split up when I was pretty young."

I slid the pan under the broiler and adjusted the temperature. As I turned, I asked, "Beer, wine, or water?"

"What are you having?"

"For the moment, water. I'll probably have a beer after we eat."

Tiffany grinned. "Perfect. I'll take water."

I filled two glasses with water, adding ice when she said she would like some. After putting the water down in front of her, I said, "I'll finish getting our food ready. But back to your question, my dad's not in Willow Brook. He and my mom never married. He was..." I shrugged. "Not the most around guy. Not a bad guy. He's up in Fairbanks now. We talk here and there, but not much. He's worked on the North Slope for years. What about your parents? You talk about your dad often, but how is your mom?"

Her expression tightened briefly before she took a deep breath and let it out in a controlled sigh. "My mom passed away."

"Oh, I'm sorry. I didn't know that."

"I wouldn't expect you to know. And thank you."

Tiffany was quiet for a few beats, and I carefully spooned some of the marinade into the seasoned rice and then stirred the vegetables in. I waited, trying to give her the space to explain or not.

"Maybe the details were different, but my mom sounds kind of like your dad. She traveled a lot when we were growing up. She and my dad weren't the happiest couple. He was the steady parent, and she wasn't. She was always looking for new jobs. We didn't have the greatest relationship." Her lips twisted as she shrugged.

"Parents aren't perfect," I offered lightly.

"Definitely not. Although my dad's awesome. He's about as close to perfect of a dad as you could get."

I grinned over at her. "Nice. My mom's about

perfect. I suppose if we get one good parent, that's lucky."

Tiffany shifted the topic after that, talking about work, asking me about firefighting, and sharing that she liked being back in Willow Brook because she could run a whole clinic. Once we were seated and eating, she took her first bite of salmon. Closing her eyes, she let out a satisfied moan.

My body tightened in reaction. I tried to tell myself she was just moaning over the food, but my body knew what Tiffany sounded like when her senses were satisfied. Her eyes opened as she finished chewing and swallowed. Fuck me.

"Fuck. This is amazing, Wes."

I almost pointed out that I would happily fuck her, but I kept my focus on the conversation. "Glad you like it."

Between dinner and cleaning up, the next half an hour or so felt like kitchen foreplay. Watching Tiffany eat was something—the flexion of her throat when her tongue darted to the corner of her mouth to swipe an errant drop of marinade, the pink on her cheeks—and all of it drove the flames higher and higher. The engine of my arousal was revving.

Then came the cleanup. She insisted that I shouldn't be part of picking up the dishes, rinsing them, and putting them in the dishwasher. All the while, my body felt like a tuning fork, solely attuned to her every motion. The subtle swing of her hips when she crossed from the sink to fetch the dish towel she left on the corner of the counter and returning to lean over and put something in the dishwasher felt like torture.

When she finally, *fucking finally*, rinsed her hands in the sink and dried them before hanging the dish towel over the handle of the dishwasher, I was at the end of my tether. It was frayed and about to snap.

She turned around, resting her hips against the counter, and announced, "There."

I pushed away from the counter where my palm had been resting on it, taking two steps to stand in front of her. I rested my hands on the counter, caging her between my arms.

Her eyes darkened as her lashes lifted to meet my gaze. Her arms were crossed. We simply looked at each other, the moment stretching out like hot liquid honey dripping from a spoon.

Her tongue darted out to slide across her lips before she took a sharp breath in. I waited.

"Is this a good idea?"

Her question fell between us, like a lit match into a field of dry grass as she put voice to the forbidden line we'd been traversing ever since our first kiss.

"I think maybe we've already gone past that point, don't you think?"

My arousal felt strained, and I could feel the press of it against my zipper.

Another slide of her tongue across her lips as she inhaled again, the sound of her breath drawing in like a lasso tightening around me.

"I guess so," she rasped.

What I said next startled me. "This isn't just about sex. I really like you, Tiffany."

Chapter Twenty-Five

WES

Tiffany's eyes widened slightly. For several thundering beats of my heart, I could sense her almost wrestling with herself. I felt as if I could see the uncertainty and questions blowing like tumbleweeds through her thoughts.

"Oh," she finally said as if she couldn't even believe it.

I'd already stumbled into this, so I committed. "Is that so surprising? The first time I saw you again when Alice came to get a dog, I thought you were sexy as hell, and I wanted you right then. I'll start with the important part. You're smart, you're funny, and you're also completely loyal to your friends and family. There's all that, *and* you're beautiful and sexy."

"Oh," she repeated, her cheeks tinged with rosy pink.

She lifted her chin, her arms unfolding and one hand lifting to catch one of her dark curls She spun it around her forefinger. "I really like you too." She bit her bottom lip as she smiled, almost bashfully. "You're smart and—"

I lifted a hand, putting a finger over her lips. "I'd rather kiss you than have you stroke my ego."

She giggled, the sound vibrating lightly against my fingertip. My hand fell away, and I stepped closer, palming her cheek as I fit my mouth over hers.

Our kiss went wild. We practically combusted as our tongues tangled, and I brought her body flush against mine. My hand slid from her cheek around to the back of her neck and down her spine to cup the lush curve of her bottom and press her against my arousal.

She arched into me, her hips rocking against the hard ridge of my arousal. I didn't even know how long we kissed, but when we broke apart, both of us were desperate for air. We stared at each other. It felt as if lightning was crackling in the air around us.

Her hand molded over my cock, sliding up and down the denim as she whispered, "I need to do this."

She turned, spinning me around and pushing me back as she deftly unbuttoned and unzipped my jeans. In another moment, I felt her palm sliding into my boxers, her touch silky smooth around my shaft. I felt a bead of pre-cum roll out the tip. She looked up at me, biting her lip as her thumb smeared it across the crown.

"Just give me a minute," she rasped. With the sly glint contained in her dark eyes, there was no way I could do anything other than exactly what she ordered.

She shoved my jeans and briefs down around my hips, and my cock sprang free. My fingers laced in her hair as she knelt. Her tongue swirled around the thick crown before she sucked my swollen length into her mouth. My head fell back, and I was grateful for the counter behind me because my knees would've given out without it.

With one hand gripping the edge of the counter and the other her hair, I gave in to the sheer torture and delirious pleasure of her sucking, licking, and stroking me. My release was threatening as my balls tightened. As much as my body wanted me to give in, I needed to be inside her.

"Tiff," I choked out. "Please wait."

I felt the subtle suction as she slowly drew back, her eyes opening as she released me with a pop. More pre-cum rolled out the tip, and I clung to my control.

"I need to be inside you," I whispered hoarsely.

She held my gaze, her look considering, almost as if she was debating whether she would even agree. In all honesty, I was truly at her mercy. Because if she drew me into her mouth one more time, that would be it for me. But she didn't. She rocked back on her heels and stood.

I took control, spinning her around and shoving her jeans down around her thighs a little roughly. She rested her elbows on the counter, and I reached around, teasing my fingers between her thighs just to make sure. I groaned at the feel of her arousal coating my fingers. She was slippery wet, and her hips rocked into my touch.

I wasn't even thinking as I slid my palm down her back, pushing her shirt up slightly. I needed to feel her skin. I fisted my cock with my other hand, just about to sink into her when I came to an abrupt stop. In my mind, it was practically the sound of tires squealing on the pavement.

"Hang on, I need to get a condom," I bit out.

Tiffany glanced over her shoulder. "I have an IUD.

There's nothing to worry about, for that or otherwise," she clarified.

We stared at each other. With my hand splayed at the base of her spine, I took a breath. "There's nothing to worry about otherwise for me either," I added. A part of our annual physical was testing for everything under the sun. I hadn't even had a casual fling since I'd moved back to Willow Brook.

"Then fuck me," she said, her voice husky.

I closed my eyes, taking a breath as blood shot straight to my cock at her blunt order.

"As you wish," I said when I opened them again.

I looked down. With her bottom tilted up, her bare pussy was pink and swollen with my cock *right* there. My eyes trailed up to the base of her spine, where my palm was splayed. I idly noticed a scar, several inches in length just a few inches above where my palm was resting. It was clearly a surgical scar.

Before I could even contemplate it, Tiffany arched, pressing her bottom back against me and her pussy sliding against my cock. "What are you waiting for?"

I shifted, finally giving in to everything I needed. I positioned my cock at her entrance and let out a growl as I slowly filled her. When I was seated fully, I rocked in, just a nudge, and took a deep breath. It wasn't simply the pure, nearly delirious feeling of being fully inside her. It felt as if I had come home, as if *this*— Tiffany, me, us, as connected as two humans could be physically—was everything.

"Wes," she gasped as her hips pushed back toward me.

That subtle motion pushed me over. It was as if a dam had broken, and the water rushed free.

Chapter Twenty-Six

TIFFANY

Wes somehow knew everything I needed. His rhythm was absolutely perfect—not too fast and not too slow but just exactly right. He interspersed subtle rocks with drawing back fully before filling me again, inch by delectable inch. I felt every sensation, the stretch of him filling me, the slick fusion of every motion, the way my thighs were pressed together from my jeans banded around them, and the sharp, piercing pleasure created by that friction.

My release was on the edge, the pleasure intensifying. Wes reached around at the exact moment I needed it, grazing his fingers over my clit. My pleasure burst like a ray of fire through me. I cried out, my channel clenching around his cock. I felt him let go as he went taut, calling my name in a rough growl. His fingers tightened on my hip, and I felt the heat of his release coming in spurts inside me.

He stayed with me until we both went still. He curled around me as we breathed together. I didn't know who moved first, but somehow, we disentangled ourselves. He lifted me into his arms, walking into the living room where he sat on the couch and held me in his lap.

———

Hours later, I woke in the darkness. I was curled against Wes's side, the human equivalent of a barnacle. One of my knees was hooked over his. My arm was curled across his stomach, and my head was tucked into the curve of his shoulder. I could feel his arm wrapped around my shoulders with his palm resting just above the curve of my bottom.

I felt safe and protected. Almost. The moment that feeling flickered into my awareness, all the voices that held my baggage, carried the heavy weight of distrust, of never believing that even good people got the love they deserved clamored to be heard. Only once before had those voices fallen silent because it was a friend, someone I thought I could trust, who had betrayed me. Just now, those voices shouted out through the haze of sleep, snapping me awake abruptly and reminding me everything was fragile. Even thinking maybe I was safe, maybe I was okay was a risk.

Those voices at this moment were powerful. Yet the need to savor the way I felt was actually stronger. Perhaps it was the darkness, or maybe it was the way Wes held me in his sleep. He was still asleep. I could feel the rhythm of his breath where my palm rested on his chest—slow and steady, following the beat of his heart.

I heard a tail swishing on the floor and smiled to myself. Nilla was mostly with Wes, but she had spent a few nights with me when Ross was there. She often wagged her tail in her sleep.

Wes shifted, not waking, but his palm moved in a soothing circle on my bottom. I almost giggled but sobered instantly. I'd gone out of my way to build a fortress around my heart, to ensure a moat and a gate and walls and battlements all aligned to keep my heart safe.

It wasn't working out that way with Wes. I'd had too much faith in myself, too much faith in those old habits.

I felt vulnerable, soft inside, as if Wes had shimmied through a crack in my defenses—not because he was trying to trap me but because I hadn't been prepared. I hadn't believed someone like him existed, not for me.

I breathed in slowly and heard another swish of Nilla's tail on the floor. Wes's palm slid halfway up my back, then back down as he mumbled something in his sleep. His arm tightened, just barely, around me, holding me even closer. Even safer.

Chapter Twenty-Seven

TIFFANY

I leaned against the tiled wall of the shower, trying to catch my breath as my heartbeat galloped and pleasure scattered through me in a shower of sparks. I dragged my eyes open to find Wes's eyes waiting.

He'd just fucked me against the wall and only a moment ago eased me down from his hold as he withdrew from me. I could see the rapid beat of his pulse at the base of his throat, his own breath coming rapidly.

"Fuck me, Tiffany," he said, his voice husky.

"You just did."

He chuckled, his head falling to rest on the curve of my neck.

Somehow, we gathered ourselves and actually took care of the business of showering. At one point, I turned, leaning my head back to rinse my hair.

Wes's hand slid down my spine smoothly because soap was still running down my back from the shampoo I'd been rinsing out of my hair when this all started.

When I lifted my head, Wes asked, "What's the scar on your back?"

His thumb traced over the scar. For a moment, I stiffened. I took a breath, letting it out quickly. "I'm fine, but I had a tumor. It's going to sound weird," I warned as I turned to face him.

He leaned back, his gaze sobering as he waited.

Because I was me and whenever I was nervous, I could launch into way too much, I gave him this long explanation.

"I started having these pains in my back, not like a muscle. They would just happen randomly it seemed. They were awful, like lightning in my body." His eyes went wide. "I know it sounds weird. Anyway, I went to the doctor, and they said I had a tumor. It was freaking terrifying because they sent me to an orthopedic oncology doctor. They assured me that maybe it was okay, but that an orthopedist surgeon needed to operate in case it was malignant. If it wasn't malignant, then I would be fine. The biopsy was hell. The poor guy told me that he was going to numb the area, but that he needed me to know that if it was a peripheral nerve sheath tumor, that I would feel it anyway. Well, that's exactly what it was, a nerve sheath tumor. It was benign." I ran out of words and took a deep breath.

Wes studied me for a moment before shaking his head. "You could've said that part first."

"I told you I was fine," I protested.

"You did, but then you started with tumor and oncology and the whole thing."

I pressed my lips together, shrugging lightly. "I guess I did."

"Do you have to worry about it coming back?"

I shook my head and shrugged at the same time.

His brows hitched up slightly. "Is that a "no" or "maybe"?"

"Probably not, but there's no guarantee," I said, trying to ignore the sneaky sense of vulnerability that slithered through me.

I didn't like how I felt when this whole thing happened. Just talking about it now reminded me that I still hadn't spoken to my father and Chase about it. I felt stupid about it. Why was I hiding this from them? I'd simply panicked when they made the original referral to an orthopedic oncologist. After hiding it, now it felt even bigger even though I was fine.

Wes nodded slowly. "There's no guarantee for anything, I suppose. You don't want to keep talking about this," he observed, the gentleness in his gaze causing my heart to twist sharply in my chest.

"No," I said honestly. "Not really."

"Do you mind that I asked?"

I shook my head quickly. "It's just weird, you know. Everything turned out okay, but it was a little scary until I knew it was benign."

"I bet."

He dipped his head, brushing a kiss along the side of my neck, his touch gentle and intimate. He tugged me away from the wall and pulled me back under the water. We finished our shower, toweled off, and got dressed. It was all very mundane. I didn't make a habit of spending the night or showering with anyone.

Until I had let my friends-with-benefits situation turn into something more, I hadn't even spent the night with a man. Sex was just sex, or that was how I'd treated it. I wasn't even sure I had loved Scott, but I *had* trusted him. I had let my feelings begin to deepen into something more. I was breaking all of my rules with Wes. The potential complications were monumental.

A little while later, we were having coffee and pancakes. I finished chewing a bite, chasing it with a swallow of coffee. "These are really good."

He waggled his eyebrows. "I'm decent in the kitchen."

I grinned. "Between dinner and this, you've proven to be more than decent. Where do you get the blueberries?"

"My mom has a bunch that grows wild in her yard. She picks them every year and freezes them."

"How's her recovery going?"

"It's going." He sighed. "She's pretty stubborn. She wants to do *all* the things before she's ready."

"It would be hard for me to rest. I get it. I'm sure you'd be the same way," I teased before taking another bite of pancake and enjoying the little burst of flavor from the blueberries scattered through them.

"Absolutely," Wes agreed.

When I smiled over at him, my heart tumbled in my chest, and I abruptly changed the subject. "Do you miss George?"

He finished his last bite and set his fork down. After he swallowed, he nodded. "I do. Couldn't see each other all that much, but we played online games weekly and texted. Whenever I log in to play with Ross now, I think about him. What about you? Do you miss Sarah?"

I nodded. "She was my best friend when we were younger. Life does get in the way, but we stayed in touch. We used to text, usually a few times a week. I still can't believe they're both gone."

A rush of emotion hit me. My throat felt tight, and

tears stung my eyes. I reached for my coffee, taking a quick swallow and savoring the sharp flavor.

"It's weird, huh?" he prompted.

His tone was understanding. When I met his eyes again, I saw grief and sadness held in his gaze and knew he understood.

"It is," I agreed. "Maybe after we weren't living in the same place, we didn't see each other that much, but she was still a presence in my life for years. Now she's gone."

"And now we have Ross."

"Should we be worried?" I blurted out.

He studied me quietly. "About us?"

I nodded jerkily.

He was quiet for several beats before offering, "Maybe we should be, but I don't want to be. This feels like something more, Tiffany."

I couldn't believe what I said next. "Maybe it feels like something more for me too." My tears were still threatening, and they weren't just about missing my old friend.

He reached across the table and curled his hand over mine, his thumb brushing across the back. "Maybe?" he teased.

I looked down at my coffee mug, tracing my thumb along the handle. "Maybe." When I lifted my eyes to his, I answered honestly, "I'm not great at relationships."

"It's not a sport." He shrugged.

His simple reply, how unworried he was, soothed and was precisely what I needed. My lips curled in a smile. "What time do we pick up Ross?"

"Archer texted me this morning that they're taking the boys cross-country skiing. He said they should be back this afternoon. Let's go do something."

Chapter Twenty-Eight

WES

"Hey, hey!" Levi Phillips said, walking past me as he clapped me on the shoulder and stopped beside me where I was standing by a table at Wildlands Bar & Restaurant.

I cast him a grin. "Hey, dude. How've you been?"

"At the moment, I'm starving," Levi said flatly.

Graham looked up from where he stood on the other side of the table. The server had just wiped it down and gestured to it. "All yours, guys."

Usually once or twice a week, a number of us firefighters met here to grab dinner and sometimes drinks. Just as I was sitting down with Graham and Levi, Russell and Rowan approached with Chase right behind them. Within a few minutes, Beck and Cade had joined us, along with Ward and Donovan. "Big group tonight," I observed.

Chase, who ended up sitting beside me, replied, "We're all starving."

"How's the baby sleeping?" Beck asked.

"Okay," Chase said. "I think. I'm trying to wake up

whenever he needs to nurse, but he always wants Hallie."

"You're not officially a feeding station," Beck offered with a wry grin.

"Beck is the parenting expert," Ward interjected.

"I'm the only one with two kids, so I've done it twice, dude."

I watched as they teased each other, relieved Chase was distracted. I sensed he was perceptive and might pick up on anything going on between Tiffany and me. Just having him around reminded me of what had passed between us, more than once now. The thing was, I was falling for her. Hell if I knew how her brother would feel about that. Although we were on the same crew together at work, work didn't mean spending a lot of downtime together, at least not yet. With it being winter, we did training exercises and occasionally subbed in for the town crew if they needed help here and there. Come summer, we'd be out fighting fires together all the time.

Our drinks and food arrived, and the conversation rolled along. We talked about the upcoming fire season and joked about who wanted to help with a new volunteer firefighter program Maisie was organizing.

Graham glanced over at Beck. "So whose idea was this volunteer program?"

Beck waggled his eyebrows. "Maisie, but not really because we used to have it before. Do you remember Carol?"

"Of course I do," Graham replied. "She was the center of the universe at the station since I was a kid. Then Maisie took over."

Beck nodded. "Carol handled the volunteer

program. The year after she passed away and Maisie was originally just filling in her position—"

Russell cut in, "She was cranky until you two got together."

Beck chuckled. "It wasn't just me. That was a rough year for her. The program kind of died on the vine, and nobody even thought to tell Maisie about it. She's been saying she wanted to get it back up and running for a while now. I will definitely be helping with it. Don't you guys break her heart by not helping."

Levi, seated beside Beck, slid an arm around Beck's shoulders, giving him a sideways back-slapping hug. "You know we'll all help. If I recall, it was a rotation before. Also, once we get the high school kids through training, they do a lot of the work as long as the calls are close to town."

Cade nodded from across the table, adding, "Their parents have to sign off. I want to say the volunteers can travel within twenty-five miles. I'll have to check. My dad would know. He helps out with it too."

Cade Masters was the superintendent for another crew, and his father was the chief of police in Willow Brook.

"I will definitely sign on to the rotation," I offered after finishing the last bite of my hamburger.

"I'm in," Chase offered from my side. He glanced at me, adding, "When they do the training exercises, I'm pretty sure you can bring Ross, right?" He directed his question back to the table in general.

"Think kids have to be ten and up," Cade replied.

"If Ross wants to do it, I'll bring him when he's old enough," I said.

A short while later, the group gradually dispersed. Chase happened to be walking out with me. I thought it was coincidental until he stopped with me at the back of my SUV.

"What's up?" I asked as I glanced over at him. A chilly gust of air came off the lake behind Wildlands Lodge. My feet crunched on the packed snow of the parking area as I turned to face him.

"How do you feel about my sister?" His tone was deceptively casual, but I sensed the thread of protectiveness laced within it.

I took a breath as I studied him, contemplating my answer. As I was gathering my thoughts, Chase added, "Hallie mentioned something was going on with you two. I think she knows more than she's telling me." His lips twisted to the side.

I steeled myself. "I like Tiffany. A lot. I don't think it's my business to talk to you about us, though. In fact, I think she's going to be rightly pissed off if she finds out you asked me anything."

Chase's chuckle was dry. "Probably. She'll definitely be pissed off at me, but I don't really care. If she's pissed off at you, well, I guess you'll have to deal with it then, won't you?"

I eyed him for a moment, lightly scuffing my toe across the ground. "Look, I didn't plan on this."

"I'm sure she didn't, either. A part of me is pissed off at you, but obviously, Tiffany's an adult. She doesn't date. To my knowledge, she's never had a serious relationship."

"Never?" I couldn't keep the surprise out of my tone.

He shook his head. "Not that I know of." He was quiet for a moment, appearing to consider his thoughts. His words were measured when he spoke again. "I don't know how much she's told you about our mom, but she did a number on us. Our dad is great, and completely solid, but things were tough with our mom. Tiffany had it even worse than I did. When our mom wanted to chase after whatever latest job, she would drag Tiffany with her, and our mom was"—Chase paused, shaking his head slightly—"confusing for a child. She ignored me more than she ignored Tiffany and then was downright harsh toward Tiffany when she was a teenager. Trust doesn't come easy to my sister. I guess that's what I'm saying."

My heart clenched. Maybe I didn't know all the details, but something about the way Chase described the situation struck me. I also recalled the guarded look that passed through Tiffany's eyes with more frequency than I wished. I already knew trust didn't come easy for her.

"Okay," I finally said, uncertain how else to reply. "I would never hurt her."

"You wouldn't mean to, but that doesn't mean you wouldn't," Chase said bluntly.

Chapter Twenty-Nine

TIFFANY

I twisted my hands together in my lap. I was over at my dad's, having dinner. Chase was stopping by to pick something up. I'd promised myself I would finally tell my dad and Chase about my surgery.

Because I was me, and whenever I got nervous, I tended to blurt things out, so I decided I was going to tell my dad first. Right this minute.

"Before I moved home last year, I thought I had cancer."

My dad had just closed the oven and turned around, oven mitt still in hand as he stared at me. "What? Are you okay? Why didn't you say anything?"

"Dad, it wasn't cancer. I'm fine."

He held my gaze for a long moment before carefully setting the oven mitt on the counter and walking over to the table to sit across from me. "What happened?" he asked.

I looked over at my father, the man who had been the mainstay in my life. My throat tightened as I recalled the times I'd wished my mother hadn't wanted to drag me with her when she chased after the latest something. Nothing ever panned out for her, or at least that was how it felt. She was always chasing something. She craved attention. She wasn't cut out to be a mother, but she'd focused on me more than Chase. It felt sort of good when we were younger, but it was mostly confusing because I never really felt good when I was with her.

I was an afterthought, something sort of annoying. She never liked being alone, so she brought me with her. When the child she'd dragged along with her was inconvenient, she would plunk me off to the side and ignore me.

My dad put a stop to it when I was about eleven years old. I would learn years later that it was after she had one of her two affairs. She'd left me alone in a hotel room for the night, and the owners had called my dad. To this day, I didn't think Chase knew that detail. I didn't even piece it together until I was older.

My dad's kind eyes waited, and my next question surprised me. "Why did you stay with her?"

Our family had been through some upheaval in the past few years with Chase discovering by chance that our father wasn't his biological father. Our mom had been with someone else when she was first dating our dad. That man was Chase's father, biologically speaking. He'd passed away before Chase knew about him.

My father had taken the news in stride and even explained it hadn't surprised him. I had initially been more invested than Chase in making those new connections. I suppose because I craved connections desperately and wanted a sense of family.

My dad studied me for a moment before nodding, as if to himself. "Because I worried if I divorced her, you and Chase might become pawns in a game for her. In hindsight, I realize I made more mistakes with you.

I should've put my foot down sooner and told her she couldn't keep taking you with her. I'm sorry for that."

Tears stung in my eyes, but I was determined not to cry. I swallowed through the achy feeling in my throat as that confusing sadness washed through me. It was a familiar feeling, one tied to my mother when she was alive. Its edges had softened after she passed away.

"It's okay," I said softly as I reached over and patted my father's hand as if I was trying to comfort him. "You put a stop to it."

My father nodded. "Eventually. I didn't see your mother clearly at first. When you and Chase were little, it was different. Or maybe I should say she really tried at first. I thought I could just handle all of it. Honestly, I suppose when you were younger, I thought maybe she would leave. I didn't realize she saw me as her only source of financial stability so she stayed. When I think back, I wish I knew what I could've changed. But even now, I don't. She was your mother and..." His words trailed off, and he shrugged, the regret and sadness in his gaze twisting an old knife in my heart.

"It's okay, Dad. I don't know what you could've changed either."

"Are you going to tell me about your cancer that wasn't cancer?" he asked gently.

I took a deep breath before letting it out and nodded. "Short version. I was having sharp pains in my back, really sharp. I went to the doctor. I panicked because they ordered an MRI and said I had a tumor. They told me I had to have a biopsy and sent me to the oncology unit to get it done because it could've been malignant. It wasn't. I was so freaked out and didn't want to freak you guys out. I just ended up not saying anything, and I don't really know why."

I didn't want to share how the guy who I'd let into my heart had let me down completely.

"Do you still have a tumor?" my dad pressed.

I shook my head quickly. "I had outpatient surgery. When they realized it was benign, they scheduled an outpatient procedure. It didn't affect my movement. It was as simple as a cyst, but it was on my spine and kind of scary at first."

My dad was saying, "I wish you would've told us," just as Chase came walking in the kitchen from the garage.

"Told us what?" he prompted.

Chase read the room quickly, picking up on the fact that we were having a serious conversation. His eyes landed on me. "What happened?" He had his keys in his hand and pocketed them as he stopped beside the kitchen table, looking back and forth between us.

"I had a benign tumor on my spine. It's fine. I had surgery to remove it a few months before moving home."

"What?" My brother's tone was sharp.

"I'm fine!" I hurried to explain. "I panicked and didn't want to scare anybody, so I didn't say anything."

Chase ran a hand through his hair, his expression bewildered as he looked at me and then back at our father. When he glanced back at me, I could feel the chill of his disappointment. "Why wouldn't you tell us about this?"

I ignored the tightness in my chest, fiddling with a napkin. I twisted it between my fingers and shrugged. "I don't know, Chase. I didn't want anybody to panic, and it turned out fine, so that made sense."

Chase looked hurt, *really* hurt. "Tiffany, you've

been home for months. You've always been so supportive of Dad and me and, well, everyone." His arm swung in an arc as if indicating the entire world.

I looked over at my father, almost desperate for him to help, to somehow explain this, to me as much as to my brother. My father, because he was the man he was, stepped into the chasm that felt like it was stretching between us. "You know, son, sometimes, things don't make a lot of sense. Especially when we're scared."

Chase stared at him before nodding very slowly as he looked back over at me.

"It doesn't make sense to me, Chase. I just panicked, and it seemed better to keep it quiet. Then I kept keeping it quiet, and it became more of a thing than it ever needed to be." I twisted the napkin even more tightly between my fingers, blinking back tears as I looked down at it.

I heard my brother take a deep breath before replying, "Okay, I get it. I'm glad you're okay. Do we need to worry?"

That weight of worry reverberated in my heart. Ever since our mother passed away, I had tried to build a bridge across the gulf she had created between Chase, my father, and me. I knew I wasn't anything like her, but those years when she had tried to make me her mini-me had been hard. I'd felt so lonely with her. As a little girl, I'd had a deeper understanding of the loneliness she felt in the world because I felt it. Her loneliness was so big. It was painful, like standing in an empty space and calling out for someone only to hear your own voice echo back to you again and again and again.

"No need to worry. I'm sorry," I said, blinking hard and swallowing before I looked up. I was an expert at not crying even when the tears were wicking up from the tight knot in my throat and stinging my eyes.

Chase took two strides. Acting on instinct, I stood, and he wrapped me in a big hug. His embrace was as sturdy and comforting as it had always been. My big brother always took care of me, or tried to, when we were kids. We had forged a strong bond, which my mother resented. I had tried to make up for the way she'd been by loving everyone as fiercely as I could.

When Chase stepped back, I felt lighter. When I looked toward my father, his soft smile felt like a beam of love.

"Are we okay?" I asked as I looked back and forth between them.

"We're always okay," Chase said firmly.

My father nodded emphatically. "Always."

A short while later, I was driving away when my dashboard lit up with the name McKenna, my brother's half-sister. Chase's discovery that he had a whole new family had been fraught for him. That had felt much easier for me because it wasn't my story. Love was big and generous when it came to everyone but me, or that was how it felt sometimes.

I tapped the screen to answer. "Hey, you!"

McKenna's voice was warm, and she replied, "Hey there!"

"What's up?"

"Just thought I'd check in. I'm planning a trip to Willow Brook for business reasons but really because it's an excuse to visit Chase and your dad and you."

"Chase mentioned you were coming."

Emotion crested like a wave inside. It wasn't this. This just reminded me of how I could deal with other people's stuff so much easier than mine. When we discovered that our dad wasn't Chase's biological father, it had been no sweat for my dad to remind Chase he was his father in every other way and really mean it. It had been a shock, but he had admitted the suspicion had always been there. Worrying about it wasn't a priority for him. While Chase had been all tied up about it and angry with our mom, which I could understand, I could handle it. I'd inherited our father's generous and loving nature and his easy acceptance of situations. Maybe I couldn't hope for love for myself, but I would give it to everyone else.

"Tiffany?" McKenna prompted.

"Oh, sorry!" I rolled my eyes to myself. "I was distracted for a minute by a moose." There *was* a moose over in a field, standing at a distance as it watched the highway. But it hadn't really distracted me, and moose were a common sighting in Alaska.

"Well, don't run into it," McKenna replied.

"Already passed it."

"Anyway, I was calling to make sure you'll be around. I texted Chase and Hallie."

"I'll be around. It'll be great to see you. Dad should be around too."

"Awesome! Well, I'll see you then."

"Let's get together, just us, while you're here."

"You got it. Also, how are things going with Ross?"

I paused, considering my thoughts for a moment. "Okay, I think. He seems to be doing all right. The whole thing is just..." I paused again. "It's just hard, I think. Both of his parents died, and now he lives in Alaska. He's got two grown-ups in charge of him who I know he doesn't remember before this."

"I know. It makes you really think about how you have to plan for contingencies. It's just sad. What do you think about them setting it up so both of you share guardianship? I think that's interesting."

"I know. Many people have more than one person listed, but I don't know what they were thinking. We're making it work."

"I think they were trying to set you up," McKenna said, her tone sly.

My internal gossip radar pinged. "What have you heard?" I ground out, sensing she and Hallie had spoken.

"Not much," she replied in a singsong voice.

"What did Hallie tell you?" I demanded.

"That means there's something to tell." She laughed, and I knew I was caught.

I gritted my teeth and let out a groan. "Fine. I kissed him, so now it's complicated, and I don't know what the hell to do because I really like him." I conveniently left out that we'd gone far past kissing.

"Good thing I'll be there. I think you and I need to get together ourselves. Just you and me. This is not a phone conversation."

I didn't know why it was so easy, but McKenna and I understood each other in a way that not everyone did. She didn't even know all the details about my mom, but she obviously knew the main part, which was that our mom had kept a big secret from our dad.

I didn't know everything about her either. She was the only sister in a whole passel of brothers. That alone would be challenging.

"We can meet at Firehouse Café the morning after you get here. You can tell me how to untangle the mess I've created for myself."

"It's a deal."

Chapter Thirty

WES

I stepped off the elliptical in the workout area at the fire station, tapping the button on it to turn it off before grabbing my water bottle and taking several swallows. When I lowered it, Rowan stepped off the other elliptical across from me.

He drained his water bottle and glanced over, cracking a grin. "How far did you go?"

"Ten miles."

"Same here. That interval thing kicks my ass sometimes."

"Isn't that the point?" I set my water bottle down as I walked over to the weights.

Rowan followed me, and we both began a rotation. "So how are things with Tiffany?" he asked between reps.

"Huh?"

He waggled his brows. "Dude, you know the way news travels in this town. There's a betting pool on whether Chase will kick your ass if you fuck this shit up. Just a heads-up on that."

I finished a series, lowering the weights and setting

them back in their stand. "For fuck's sake," I muttered.

"You've got this. Just plan on marrying her, and you'll be all set."

"Marrying her?" I sputtered.

He set his weights down, shrugging as he straightened. "Just don't break her heart." His gaze sobered as he looked at me. He clearly sensed my internal confusion. "You okay?"

"I think I'm in over my head."

"All right, this calls for an actual conversation."

A short while later, we had showered and changed and were in the kitchen at the station. I was relieved Chase wasn't around. A few more guys were now working out, and some others were watching TV. Even though we didn't hang out and spend the night here, we had a pretty nice setup.

Blessedly, it was just Rowan and me in the kitchen area at the moment. I got us two bottles of water, and he fetched some chips from the snack area before sitting at the table. After he settled in, he circled his hand in the air. "Okay, spill."

"Spill what?" Beck approached from the hallway area, snagging his own bottle of water and some chips before sitting and looking at me expectantly.

I groaned as I glanced back and forth between them. "Dude, do you ever not just jump into any conversation?" I couldn't help but ask.

Unrepentant, Beck shook his head. Rowan cracked a grin, shaking his head slightly as his gaze flicked from Beck to me. "He's like that. You just gotta get used to it."

Beck shrugged, offering, "Maybe I'm nosy..." He paused when Rowan snorted, and I rolled my eyes. "I give good advice." He looked at Rowan. "Wouldn't you say?"

Rowan eyed him thoughtfully. "Actually, yes." Pausing, Rowan gestured to me. "Wes thinks he's in over his head."

Beck leaned his elbows on the table. "Did you do something stupid?"

I smiled ruefully before taking a swallow of water. Setting the water bottle down, I traced around the base of it with my forefinger as I considered his question. "Yes. I definitely did something stupid. Then I compounded it by doing something more stupid. Maybe none of it would matter, except I'm unexpectedly in charge of a kid."

Beck's gaze shifted from teasing to somber. It was sometimes amusing to consider the Beck I knew growing up here. When he was younger, he was always in the middle of something. He was the first kid to take a dare and sort of the class clown, but never an asshole about it. In high school, he'd been a serious flirt. Again, not an asshole, but not the kind of guy anyone expected to be serious. In the years I'd been away, aside from becoming a hotshot firefighter, Beck had fallen in love, gotten married, and had two kids. He was a dedicated family man who loved his wife and his kids with unabashed fierceness. Family life suited him. Oh, he was still a flirt and a tease and always quick with a dare and the aforementioned nosy guy who injected himself into any conversation, but he was always good-natured and solid and loyal as a friend in all aspects.

"You're a father," he said. "Even if it doesn't seem like that."

I leaned back in my chair, running a hand through my hair and letting my arm drop as the weight of what he said slammed into me. "How can I be a father? Ross's dad just died. Obviously, I know I'm his guardian, but..." My words trailed off as I looked at my two friends, feeling a little lost about it all.

"That's not it. I get it, man. Maybe it's not there emotionally yet, but you're the guy making the major decisions in this kid's life."

Rowan nodded. "True. The emotional part will catch up, but you're it for this kid. You and Tiffany."

Beck leaned back in his chair, cocking his head to the side as he studied me. "Something's going on with you and Tiffany," he said, without even a little bit of doubt in his question. His words were spoken as a statement, a fact.

Rowan pressed his tongue on the inside of his mouth, a hint of mirth entering his gaze. "Yeah."

I groaned, muttering, "Fuck."

"We're friends," Rowan said by way of explanation. "He didn't say much to me about it, just that Hallie mentioned something to him."

"Did he talk to you?" Beck interjected.

I nodded, letting out a resigned sigh. "Yeah. And that's why I fucked up. I'm in over my head. I didn't mean for this to become a thing. I really like Tiffany. Neither one of us planned for this, and it wouldn't be a big deal except—"

"For Ross," Beck finished for me. "Last thing that kid needs is for the two new people in charge of his whole universe to get complicated."

"Fuck." Rowan let out a low laugh, shaking his head slowly. "I guess the upside is you really like her. How does she feel?"

"I think we're on the same wavelength, but I'm not sure."

"Do you love her?" Beck was dead serious, his eyes

on mine as he waited for my answer.

My heart thudded in my chest, kicking hard and fast. Beck dropping that word—love—like it was no big deal, yet also *everything*, felt like a kick straight in my solar plexus.

"Oh, man," Rowan said as he studied me.

"What?" I looked between them.

"You love her," Beck said, stating it as fact, his voice level and steady.

"What the hell?" I sputtered. "I think it's a little soon for that."

I glanced at Rowan as if he would clear up that little misunderstanding.

All he did was shrug. He looked toward Beck. "I don't think he's ready to face the facts yet."

"How the hell can you guys know if I'm in love?" Defensiveness bristled inside me.

"We probably know more than you do about love," Beck said dryly. He thumbed toward Rowan. "This guy was in love with Mae since college. He always knew she was the one. It just took a while for them to sort that out. Maybe I didn't know what love felt like, but I knew when I knew. Maisie is *it* for me." Beck thumped his fist against his chest, and the certainty in his words and eyes felt like a bell ringing in my own chest.

I leaned forward on my elbows, tunneling my hands through my hair before dropping them to the table as I let my breath out. "Wow." My voice was wondering.

"Don't fuck it up," Beck warned me.

"Setting aside whether I'm in love with Tiffany, which I'm not so sure about, what the hell do I do about Ross?"

"Tighten your shit up with Tiffany before you guys

talk to him about it. And don't be stupid. He's already been through enough."

"I know." My heart gave an achy thump as I thought of my friend George and the fact that he was just gone.

Rowan looked at me. "Talk to Tiffany first," he said quietly.

TIFFANY

"Okay," I said as I eyed the computer screen. "Looks like Moose has his rabies shot due in two months." I looked up at the woman waiting at the counter.

"Can we go ahead and schedule his appointment for that?"

"You got it." I tapped into the schedule.

A few minutes later, we had him scheduled, and they departed. Just after a woman with a very irate cat went into the back for her appointment, I glanced up to see my brother walking in with his dog Jasper.

"Oh, hey," I said as I stood. "I didn't know you had an appointment today for Jasper."

Chase looked down at his fluffy white dog and back up at me. "We didn't." He gestured to Jasper, and I glanced down to see the dog's nose full of porcupine quills. Jasper looked very uncomfortable.

"Oh, sweetie," I said as I knelt beside him. Sad eyes blinked up at me.

"Does Alice have time to see him?" he asked.

"She'll fit him in," I said as I straightened. "She's with a cat in the back right now. As soon as they're done, she has an hour break because a family was supposed to bring in two dogs for their annual exams, but they canceled because of a work conflict. I guess your timing is good. I'll be right back." I held a finger up. "I'll check and see how long she'll be."

I walked into the back. Conveniently, Alice was walking out of the exam room to get something out of the supply room. "Chase is here with Jasper. Porcupine quills."

"Oh no!" Alice's palm flew to her chest. "I'll fit him in. We're going to need to sedate him."

"How long will you be?"

"I should be done in about five minutes." She glanced at the clock on the wall. "Farrah will be in soon, right?"

"She gets here in a half hour." We had hired a vet tech to come in for the afternoons.

I returned to the front to update Chase. A short while later, Farrah arrived and came out to get Jasper. "He'll be fine." I heard her assuring Chase.

"What kind of name is Farrah?" Chase asked after he returned to the front.

I snorted. "Apparently, her parents were fans of Farrah Fawcett."

His mouth dropped open. "Are you freaking kidding me?"

"Nope." I giggled. "She can roll with it. Feel free to tease her."

Chase shook his head slightly before pushing away from the counter and stuffing his hands in his pockets as he paced back and forth in front. "Jasper will be fine. It didn't look like there were too many quills."

He turned, facing me. "I know. I just hope he's not in too much pain." He abruptly changed the subject. "I talked to Wes."

"What?" I yelped.

"Yeah," he replied as if it was perfectly okay for him to nose into my personal life.

"Chase!" I sputtered. "My personal life is my business."

My brother rolled his eyes. "Says the woman who noses into my life all the freaking time. Look, maybe it isn't any of my business, but we both have our own baggage around Mom, and I don't want to see my friend make things worse for you."

Chase stating the obvious so plainly felt like someone dragging a rusty nail over the scars on my heart. He didn't even know about what happened with Scott.

I took a slow breath. "I can take care of myself."

"Can you? Because it seems to me your way of doing that is to never get serious with anyone."

Defensiveness sharpened its claws inside. "You're one to talk," I retorted. "You didn't get serious with anyone until Hallie got pregnant."

Unperturbed, he shrugged. "You're right. That's exactly what happened, and I feel lucky. I love Hallie."

My chest and throat hurt. Despite the old, achy pain his words elicited, I was determined not to cry in front of him. "Sure. Easy for you to say. It was way worse for me, and you know it. With you, she just ignored you. With me, she spent years dragging me all over the place and then lashed out at me when I wasn't exactly how she wanted me to be, or when I got old enough for her to think I was some kind of competition."

Chase looked horrified. "Tiffany, I didn't mean—"

I shook my head sharply. "It's fine, it's fine." If I said that enough, it would somehow be true. "I didn't mean to say all that. It's just it *was* a little different for us. And you know what? I'm so happy for you and Hallie. I'm just trying to figure this out with Wes. Maybe it was stupid because of Ross."

My brother studied me quietly, the understanding held in his gaze making me want to look away. But I lifted my chin and held his gaze, stupidly proud that my tears didn't spill over.

"You've always had such a big heart. Mom didn't ruin that for you. I'm just realizing now that you don't give yourself much. You deserve love too, you know? When everything happened around Dad and the family I didn't know I had, you were the first to try to make those connections and smooth everything over. Frankly, if it wasn't for you, I don't know that I ever would've made the connection. I'm so grateful I did. Just give yourself a chance. Maybe I overstepped by saying something to Wes. I just don't want to see you hurt more."

I lost the fight against my tears. They rolled down my cheeks as I stared at my brother across the counter. He came around the counter and pulled me into his arms, giving me a big comforting hug. He stepped back, his hands on my shoulders as he stared into my eyes.

"I won't butt in again. I mean, I will kick his ass if he hurts you. But for what it's worth, Wes is a good guy."

Chapter Thirty-Two

WES

"Nice to meet you," McKenna Cannon said.

I moved to shake her hand, but her smile widened, and she stepped closer, throwing her arms around me in an enthusiastic hug. "Nice to meet you too." I chuckled as she stepped back.

"You're family now," she added.

"I am?"

"Well, yes. You and Tiffany have Ross. And Tiffany is Chase's sister, and Chase is our brother. They're family, so you're family."

Chase approached, handing me a bottle of beer. "McKenna's definition of family is very broad," he offered with a dry laugh.

Tiffany had filled me in on the family situation with them discovering a few years prior that the father who raised her and Chase wasn't Chase's biological father. The Cannon family, who owned Fireweed Industries and also happened to be one of the most well-known families in Alaska along with running an international billion-dollar company, were the other half of Chase's family.

I imagined that had been a lot for Chase to take in, but they all seemed to have settled into accepting it. McKenna was one of his seven—count that, seven—half-siblings from his biological father's side of the family.

McKenna and Chase shared the same dark blond hair and silver-gray eyes. She was quiet for a beat before her lips curled into a soft smile. "Family is what you make it. I know that's kind of a cliché and popular to say these days, but it's true. What matters is accepting each other and being there for each other." She looked from Tiffany to me and then over at Ross, who was currently occupied with playing video games. "If you need anything, all you have to do is give a shout."

A little while later, we were eating casually from a buffet-style dinner Chase and Hallie had set up. McKenna was explaining, "So Archer has been insanely busy with the transition from the old mining operation to turn it into a renewable energy operation. He's been coordinating with Off The Grid in Diamond Creek."

"It's basically a new business," I commented. "I know the town is glad Fireweed Industries is keeping part of the business here."

McKenna glanced over, nodding in agreement. "Absolutely. We already had the property and the offices. Archer's doing a massive retrofit. Otherwise, we would've been scouting for a new site. In the long run, this is more cost effective for Fireweed Industries. It also helps repair some frayed ties in the community. There was a lot of opposition to the mine." She let out a sigh.

"Why were they going to reopen the mine

anyway?" Hallie asked. She'd put their baby son to bed only a few minutes earlier.

McKenna glanced over, rolling her eyes. "Our asshole uncle ran this branch before Archer took over. That's why he and Phoebe got married." She noticed the confused look on my face and grinned. "They're totally in love. They were best friends forever when they were little."

"I recall," I said. "So what's the deal?"

"My grandparents set up this weird thing that for Archer to take over completely, he had to be married. Although it sounds weird and old-fashioned, it's not that wildly unusual in larger companies because, statistically speaking, marriages indicate stability. But he had a time-frame. Fortunately, he and Phoebe fell in love in the nick of time and got married so our asshole uncle was pushed out. The situation opened up a can of worms around the fact that he had been embezzling money. He's currently facing charges for that. He wanted to reopen the mine and kicked up a political storm over it. Fireweed Industries has been beloved in Alaska for a long time, and that was one of the worst public relations nightmares we had to deal with. I run the public relations department." She threw her hands up, letting them fall.

Tiffany chimed in, "That must've been fun."

McKenna shrugged. "Mostly annoying. That's why I'm here. I'm coordinating with Archer's team to get press releases organized about the new renewable energy offices. Off The Grid has a stellar reputation here and internationally. They're way ahead of the curve with developing new renewable energy products, so it's a mutually beneficial partnership."

As the night carried on, it became increasingly difficult for me to keep my focus off Tiffany. Tiffany drew my attention. She was the flame, I was the moth, and I didn't even care if I got burned.

She was seated beside me, with her dark hair pulled up in a twist and tendrils dangling along the sides of her neck and around her cheeks. I wanted to dust kisses along the sensitive skin of her neck because I knew it made her shiver. I wanted to undo that tidy twist and bury my fingers in her silky hair. I wanted the feel of her gasping and whimpering as she arched against me.

Someone clearing their throat snapped me out of my need-filled reverie. I whipped my gaze up to find Chase giving me a hard stare. I gave him a bland smile and took a swallow of my beer, draining it before lowering it and idly spinning the bottle between my fingers.

Ross was staying with me for the weekend. Tiffany and I had settled into a schedule that seemed to be working. We were still talking with the therapist about whether one of us should be the primary, although with my work schedule, it seemed best to keep it somewhat flexible.

Ross still hadn't cried about his parents, at least not in front of me or Tiffany. We had both talked about it and checked with the therapist about it. She'd given us information about grief for children his age and emphasized how grief was an individual process. She had also pointed out more than once that this was all very overwhelming for him, and the shock and numbness of it might still be protecting him from the intensity of his feelings about the loss of his parents.

Later that night, back at my house, Ross was sitting on the floor petting Nilla. I finished tidying up the kitchen and closed the dishwasher before tapping it to start. When I walked into the living room, Ross looked up, his eyes curious. "Do you like Tiffany?" he asked, catching me off guard.

I felt my eyes widen and quickly tried to school my expression to neutral. I scrambled inside for how to respond, settling on, "Of course I like Tiffany. She's my friend. We both grew up in Willow Brook, so we've known each other for years."

All of those things were true, so I hoped my answer was good enough.

Ross looked down at Nilla, watching the path of his hand as he dragged it through the fur along her back. "I saw you kissing her." He looked up again.

Fuck my life. Now I had to come up with some kind of answer about this. Ross was smart. He would pick up on it if I tried to skirt the issue.

I took a breath, considering my answer and wishing I had time to call Tiffany.

Ross saved me. He studied me for a moment before adding, "You don't have to explain. It's okay. I know kissing is a grown-up thing. That's what my mom and dad said."

I started to reply, but he suddenly started crying. He buried his face in Nilla's neck. Nilla sat up, leaning against him. She knew he was hurting and just let him lean on her and cry.

While I felt uncertain about how to respond, I waited. When his sobs finally quieted, I asked, "Do you want to talk about it?"

He shook his head into Nilla's neck. She was curled protectively around him.

"Okay. Let me know if you want to talk about it, and I'll listen. I want you to know I miss your dad too," I said quietly.

Ross nodded into Nilla's neck, turning his head to the side as he replied, "He talked about you because he played video games with you. He said you were his best friend from college."

"We were best friends. I'll always miss him even though I didn't see him that much. We talked every week when we played."

Unsure what else to say, I crossed over and sat on the couch nearby. After a few more minutes, Ross lifted his head from Nilla, dragging his sleeve across his face. I watched as he took a deep breath before he looked over at me, blinking and offering, "I'm okay."

After Ross went to bed, I lay in bed, propped against some pillows as I pondered whether to text Tiffany about his question about us kissing.

Lifting my phone, I figured I might as well because at least I could warn her. I also wanted to let her know he had finally said something about his parents. As much as that made my heart ache, that was easier to approach with her than him asking about us kissing. That topic felt fraught.

Me: *Ross said he missed his parents tonight and cried. He said he didn't want to talk more about it. Nilla was a big help.*

Tiffany: *Oh, wow. I'm glad he was with Nilla. He's really bonded with her. Dogs are better than humans for listening. I'm glad you were there too.*

Me: *Also, he told me he saw us kissing and asked me if I liked you.*

Staring at my phone screen, there was a pause before I saw the dots appear, indicating she was typing.

Tiffany: *Fuck. What did you say?*

Me: *First, he asked me if I liked you. I said yes and that we've known each other for years because we grew up together. Then he told me he saw us kissing, basically calling me out for trying to avoid the topic.*

Tiffany: *What did you say when he said he saw us kissing?*

Me: *He saved me by telling me I didn't have to explain, that he knew kissing was a grown-up thing.*

Tiffany: *We need a better answer than that.*

Me: *I'd love any suggestions.*

Tiffany: *I don't have any. We need to talk.*

Me: *Now?*

Tiffany: *I'm exhausted. Not now. I'll call you. Sleep well.*

Me: *Good night, then.*

I tried to ignore the sense of disappointment that slipped through me. I wanted to talk to her tonight. Just because of scheduling and Ross and life, we hadn't had a night together in more nights than I wanted to contemplate. I missed her.

Tiffany: *Good night.*

My fingers itched to say more, to tell her I missed her and I was falling for her. I didn't know if she was ready to hear any of that yet.

I recalled Chase's warning to me that Tiffany had issues with trust and I'd better not hurt her.

Chapter Thirty-Three

TIFFANY

"So Wes?" McKenna prompted.

I lifted my eyes from the menu, colliding with her knowing gaze. "What about Wes?" I sidestepped.

"He's totally got the hots for you. He's not my type, but he is hot." She gave me an exaggerated brow waggle.

Heat flashed into my cheeks. I wanted to ignore her and pretend it was nothing, but McKenna and I were pretty close. We had connected easily, and there was a benefit that she didn't live in Willow Brook, so confiding in her was a little safer. Not that I didn't trust most of my friends, but because it was hard to keep anything quiet here.

I ignored the fiery burn on my cheeks and held McKenna's gaze. "Like I mentioned, I'm worried it's complicated." The teasing look in her eyes faded. "I like Wes. A lot. Probably too much, and we made the mistake of—" I paused, stumbling as I tried to come up with a word to define the lightning strike of chemistry between us.

"Falling for his hotness," McKenna interjected helpfully.

I snorted a laugh, gathering myself. Anxiety spun in my chest. I felt tangled in a net of my own making. "It's complicated. We have Ross to consider, and he doesn't need complicated."

The moment got somber instantly. McKenna considered me quietly before nodding. "I understand that concern. I'm confident you're not alone in your feelings. I saw the way he looked at you the other night. Have you talked about it with Wes?"

Emotion roared forward, throwing me off balance mentally. "A little. He thinks it's worth the risk."

"And you don't?" McKenna pressed.

I blinked at the sudden rush of tears in my eyes. I had never planned to fall for anyone and sworn up, down, sideways, and upside down that it was never worth it. I wasn't sure I had what it took to trust. In romance, for me, the mental trust fall exercises never worked. I believed I would fall, and no one would ever be there to catch me. The one time I'd let down my guard, that was precisely what happened.

That was all too much to explain right now. Even though McKenna had pieces of that story because she also learned many years too late that she had a half-brother, none of us would ever know the whole truth because my mother didn't tell us. It was just as likely that she didn't know who Chase's father was. Much as I didn't want to give my mother credit for anything, in this scenario, it was most likely that she suspected my father was Chase's father. Because if she thought she could convince Jacob Cannon that he was the father of her child, she would've gone for it. She would've wanted the money and the prestige of being connected to the family.

As those thoughts bounced against each other like unruly bumper cars in my mind, I looked over at McKenna and shrugged. "We've talked. A little. I'm just worried. I have too many of my own issues when it comes to relationships. We have to focus on Ross, and we can't let our own baggage get in the way."

McKenna's brow furrowed with worry. "Why don't you think it's worth it? My gut tells me it is. Wes seems like a really nice guy. I asked Phoebe about him. She said he's totally solid, and he used to be kind of a nerd. He's a totally sexy hotshot firefighter now."

I rolled my eyes. "Is there some kind of rule that says if someone's a nerd, they're not an asshole?" I teased, trying to knock this conversation off track.

I had already made my decision, but I didn't want to be talked out of it. I was going to tell Wes we needed to slow this runaway train down. We needed to put a pause on things, especially those crazy kisses. Because my craving for everything I never thought I could have was getting overwhelming and threatening to swamp me.

McKenna didn't take the bait. She arched a brow, her mouth twisting to the side as she replied dryly, "No rule on that. Back to my point, Wes seems like a good guy."

———

The weekend passed in a blur. I saw Wes two more times. With McKenna and others joining us, we went on a snowshoe hike to a frozen waterfall nearby. Later that night, Ross was with me, and Nilla was waiting by the hallway to go to bed. I glanced over at her, smiling. "She knows the schedule," I offered.

Ross grinned. A few minutes later, he'd brushed his

teeth and changed for bed. I peered into his bedroom to see Nilla curled up beside him with him leaning against the headboard with a book. He liked to read. His serious gaze lifted to meet mine.

"Good night," I said. "Sleep tight."

He opened his mouth to say something before he looked down quickly, curling a hand and knuckling a tear that rolled down his cheek.

"Are you okay?" I hurried into the room, sliding my hips onto the bed just as Nilla shimmied closer and rested her chin on his shins.

Ross's head stayed bowed. "I think so," he said with a sniffle. "I've been missing my mom and dad."

I ignored the rush of anxiety. Wes and I had talked together and individually with Ross's therapist about preparing for these moments. I'd practiced what I would say to myself time and again. Because I had to say the right thing. I couldn't screw this up.

"You're going to miss them," I said, striving to keep my tone level and soothing even though I felt a little panicked inside.

He lifted his head and studied me quietly. "Is this okay?"

"That you miss your parents?"

Nilla wiggled even closer, close enough for Ross to bury his hand in her fur. His book slipped off his lap.

Ross shook his head. "That I'm here. That you and Wes are—" He paused, chewing on the inside of his cheek. "In charge of me, like my mom and dad, I guess."

"Of course it's okay." I moved to sit closer, curling an arm around his shoulders as I leaned against the headboard beside him. "Both of us want to take care of you. Your parents were our best friends. Maybe we didn't know you that well because we lived in different places, but we made a promise because we cared. We're not just doing this because. We're doing it because it matters. You matter."

I could feel the tension reverberating through him. He softened slightly, his head falling forward again. I let my arm shift, my palm sliding in a smooth circle in the center of his back. "I know we talked about it with your therapist, but we hope it's okay that you have both of us. We hope that we've worked out a way for this to be extra. If you prefer to be at one place more, all you need to do is say so."

He shook his head as he peered up at me. "I like it this way. It's extra."

That was the word we had come up with to describe that he had both of us. Both places, both families.

My lips curled in a soft smile. "It is extra."

"I told Wes it's okay that you kissed," he mentioned.

I almost choked. I willed the heat rising up my neck and creeping into my cheeks away. "Okay," I squeaked, silently cursing.

Ross saved me after that, changing the subject and talking about school and Nilla and wanting to go snowshoeing again.

When I fell asleep a short while later, I resolved to talk to Wes.

Chapter Thirty-Four

WES

I stared at Tiffany, taking in her tousled curls, the bright blue of her eyes, and the way her mouth was set in a tense line. She was determined, and I wanted to argue the point anyway.

"Tiffany, all it takes is giving *this,* giving *us* a chance. You mean more to me than that."

Tears glistened in her eyes as her curls swung when she shook her head. "It's not about what it takes for us. We have to think of Ross first," she insisted.

"I understand. I'm trying to say that I think we can have it all."

She stared at me, her eyes going wide. The doubt was so evident that my heart ached.

"Did I do something for you not to trust me?"

Tiffany shook her head. "It's not you—"

I cut in, "Don't you dare tell me it's not you, it's me. What the hell happened?"

"It isn't you," she retorted, her mouth twisting with annoyance as she drummed her fingertips on the table. We were meeting for coffee at Firehouse Café, and I'd all but forgotten we were in a public place. "Look, I don't talk about it much, but you know my dad. He's awesome, but my mom treated him like shit. The thing with Chase was just the icing on the cake of her being unavailable for us emotionally. When I was little, she dragged me all over while she ran around trying to get something that would make her famous. I was always bouncing around. Then she had two affairs." Tiffany closed her eyes. When she opened them, the bitterness there felt like a spear being driven through my heart. "Trust just isn't a thing that comes easy for me. I know that being decent doesn't mean getting a good person to love you. My dad is one of the most decent human beings I've ever known. My surgery?"

"What about it?"

"I'd started dating a guy I'd been friends with. I only trusted him because we were friends first. Both of us started to have feelings for each other, or so I thought. I thought maybe it was worth giving it a shot. As soon as the possibility of cancer floated on the horizon, he ghosted me." Tiffany swallowed. I could feel her willing herself not to cry, and it broke my heart. "Don't feel sorry for me," she ordered. A hardness I'd never seen entered her gaze as she stared at me. "So if we let this go somewhere and it doesn't work out, I don't know if I can handle it. I just don't know if I can."

She glanced around the café, which was bustling with people, all of them oblivious to our conversation over here in the corner. She'd texted me this morning, asking if we could meet for coffee. I'd stupidly thought she just wanted to see me.

"I have to go." She thrust her arms into her jacket, which hung over her chair. She looped her purse over her shoulder as she stood, her hand curling tightly around the leather strap. "Let's not have this get weird. Ross knows we kissed, but he doesn't need to know anything more or worry about anything getting weird."

She walked away swiftly. I sat at the table, feeling almost emotionally shell-shocked. I took a swallow of my coffee, almost by habit. "Do you need anything else?" A voice reached me, puncturing my emotional stupor.

I glanced up to see Janet smiling down at me. The moment she saw my face, she reached out, placing her hand on my shoulder. "Are you okay?"

I took a quick breath, scrambling for some composure as I nodded. "I guess. I just got dumped."

"Oh!" Janet's hand flew to her chest. "You love her."

I stared at Janet as my heart began kicking up a racket against my ribs. "I guess I do," I said slowly. "She's worried it will mess things up for Ross."

Janet sat across from me, sliding the tray with a few empty coffee cups onto the top of the table between us. "That's a reasonable concern. Does she know how you feel?"

"I think so."

"You *think* so?" she prompted, her tone skeptical.

"I told her this really matters to me, that I wanted us to give it a chance."

"Did you tell her specifically that you love her?"

I pressed my tongue on the inside of my cheek, idly picking up my fork and rocking it between my fingers. "Not specifically," I finally said.

Janet's gaze softened as she studied me. "Tiffany has plenty of reasons not to trust. None of them have anything to do with you, but you might need to build a bridge strong enough for her to cross safely."

I let my breath out in a ragged sigh. "Ah. So I'm going to have to put myself out there?"

"Oh, yes," Janet said with a firm nod.

I sighed again. "I guess I thought I was already doing that."

Janet smiled softly. "Sometimes that's what you have to do. That's not to say you're responsible for her baggage, but if you love her, you have to try to under-stand it. We all come with baggage. Tiffany is one of those people who has a big heart. She's sensitive and goes out of her way for the people she cares about. The flip side to that is she has a lot to protect."

Chapter Thirty-Five

WES

I mulled over Janet's advice later that night. Ross and I played online video games with Chase, and Ross kicked both of our asses. We were just turning everything off, and Ross still had the video game controller in his hands when he glanced over at me.

"What?" I asked reflexively.

Ross blinked up at me before offering, "I know I said grown-up kisses are none of my business, but you really like her."

I had stood to put my controller in the drawer. While Nilla was a sweetheart, we had discovered she was nosy when it came to things staying out. I turned, feeling flat-footed as I stared at him. "Uh-huh."

This little boy, who seemed too old for his years, simply stared back at me before shrugging. "Don't be dumb."

With that, he stood from the couch and walked over to place his controller in the drawer and shut it. He dusted his hands on his jeans as if he had just finished a hard job before adding, "Good night."

Without another word, he turned. Nilla leaped off the couch to trot behind him down the hallway.

I was starting to feel like the biggest idiot in the classroom here.

I wanted to say it was on a whim, but it wasn't. Emotion was rushing through me, a tide that just kept rising. Maybe an hour later, after Ross was in his bedroom with the lights out and presumably asleep, I was still in the living room. I had brushed my teeth and intended to go to bed, but I was too restless.

I lifted my phone, sliding my thumb across the screen and pulling up Tiffany's number. We frequently texted, usually daily, but for some reason, that had slowed over the past few days.

I called her. The moment the phone started ringing in my ear, nervous anticipation spun in my chest, tightening around my heart as my gut churned with it.

I prayed she didn't answer while also praying that she did. Because I needed to say what I felt.

The phone clicked, and her voicemail played. *"Hey, it's Tiffany. Leave a message and I'll call you back. Maybe."* Her tone was light and teasing.

My lips curled in a smile simply at the sound of her voice.

I spoke in a rush. "Hey, it's me. I need to say this in person, but I'm saying it now so I don't back out." I laughed a little nervously. "I know you're worried about what this means for Ross. He's my priority too. But I love you, and that's not going to change. I want to make this work. I'm not trying to pressure you. I guess I think it's important that you know how I feel." I paused again, uncertain of what else to add.

"That's it. That's the message. I love you."

I tapped to end the call and lowered the phone.

My heartbeat was thundering in a rolling drumbeat through my body. My hands were sweating, and my breath felt short.

I set the phone down on the coffee table and took several slow breaths, trying to quell the emotion rushing through me and driving my heartbeat forward. I stared at my phone, wondering if Tiffany would even play my message tonight or if she was awake.

She didn't text or call that night.

I could've been upset. I could've wished I hadn't left that message. But I wasn't. I said what I needed to say.

Chapter Thirty-Six

TIFFANY

I replayed Wes's message, ending with, *I love you*.

My heart felt like it was going to break through my rib cage as I stared at the phone. It was a weekday, and he and I were supposed to meet at the school for parent-teacher conferences. It was really weird. I was functioning as a parent, even if I didn't fully grasp the role and even if it hadn't happened the usual way. I'd always been the person who believed family was what you made it.

I thought about my father's reaction to learning Chase was not his biological son. To him, that had been an irrelevant detail. What was important was the relationship they had and that he'd been a father in the emotional sense for the entirety of Chase's life.

Now, the idea of going to this parent-teacher conference with Wes had me in a near-panic state. I was almost afraid to face him. I was almost afraid to say aloud what my heart knew to be true. I'd fallen in love with him too. So why wasn't I thrilled he loved me?

I stood nervously from my kitchen table, hurrying

into the shower. I felt restless inside, shying away from the truth and my emotions. I knew why. I was too afraid it wouldn't hold. I was too afraid it wouldn't matter. I was too afraid that maybe somewhere inside me I shared that flighty quality my mother had, that deep uncertainty that drove her to constantly look for something else to fill it.

Roughly an hour later, I parked outside the school and got out of my car quickly, not letting myself wait or hesitate. I would face Wes. I would tell him that I still needed some time.

The school meeting was actually okay. Although I felt Wes's questioning gaze on me a few times, we both played it cool. Ross was doing well in school, so the meeting was mostly a formality.

At the end of the meeting, his teacher glanced back and forth between us. "I have to say, the two of you have done an incredible job. It sounds like this was unexpected for both of you, and while this is an unconventional arrangement for guardianship, it's working out well for Ross. He has a support network between both of your families and both of you working together. I'm really grateful you didn't hesitate." She paused, glancing toward Wes. "With your job, it's an ideal situation since you're gone for stretches of time."

Wes nodded, clearing his throat before he replied, "I am. We're kind of doing this by the seat of our pants, but we're glad it's going okay."

When he glanced at me, all I could do was nod. Emotion felt lodged in my throat. I managed to thank the teacher and was grateful she didn't have time to linger. I felt the urge to bolt when we were walking down the hallway. The bell rang just as we reached the door. The hallway went from quiet to the doors opening and kids hurrying out to go wherever they went next. I was almost relieved for the interruption because it masked my urge to flee.

I arrived before Wes, but he'd parked his vehicle beside mine. There were only so many spots to choose from, but I felt frustrated. I wanted to escape.

Get a fucking grip. No matter what, you have to deal with him.

All these years later, I wondered if this was how my mother used to feel about my father. I would never know if she actually loved him.

A voice whispered in the distance. *You love Wes. Give him a chance. Give yourself a chance.*

I blinked, willing the sting of tears away.

Stopping by my car, I curled my hand around the door handle when Wes's voice caught me, snagging like a hook along the ragged edges of my heart.

"Tiffany."

I turned, my hand still curled around the door handle. As if it could keep me from flying away and spinning into the storm of my emotions.

"Yeah?" My voice came out a little rough.

He studied me for a moment before stepping closer and lifting a hand to brush a loose lock of hair off my cheek and tuck it behind my ear. His fingertips were warm. The subtle brush of them along the outer shell of my ear and the sensitive skin behind it sent a fiery shiver through me.

His hand dropped away as his gaze coasted over my face. My heartbeat drummed a nervous echo.

"I'd ask you if you got my message, but I think you did. You don't have to reply. I just wanted to say it face-to-face. I love you."

His words fell softly between us. He waited for a beat, and I couldn't even speak.

"I'll let you think about it. I'd like to give us a chance to give this a chance." He curled his hand in a fist, pressing it to his chest before unfurling it and placing his palm directly over my heart.

"Okay," I whispered through the thick knot of emotion in my throat, praying I didn't burst into tears right in front of him. I felt split in two inside—one part of me nearly jumping for joy at his words and the love held in his eyes, and the other part nearing a panic attack, overwhelmed with fear and the desire to run away from all of this.

He waited for another moment before he stepped back, saying, "I know what you mean about Ross, and I'll give you space. Just think about what I said."

I watched as he walked away, feeling utterly bereft and gutted. That restless urge to flee thrummed through my body, mingling with a desire to chase after Wes, to grab him with both hands and tell him I loved him too, tell him he was everything I wanted.

Instead, I held the door handle and watched as he climbed into his SUV and drove away.

TIFFANY

I studied at my computer screen at work, playing shuffleboard with Alice's and the new vet tech's schedule. Farrah had fit right in here. She picked up many of the appointments for routine shots and other issues Alice could pass off. We were busy enough that I knew we needed to look into getting a second vet tech and possibly hiring another veterinarian. Alice wasn't ready to go there yet, but I was prepared to talk her into it sometime soon.

The chime above the door in the waiting area rang out. I finished making one change before glancing up to see Mr. Green, my favorite high school teacher, walking through the door with a cat carrier in hand. The moment I saw him, bitterness chased through me.

I deeply resented the fact that Mr. Green, a man I'd looked up to and trusted, ended up having a fling with my mother. I also hated that I knew this. It was only one weekend, but it still happened.

I had long ago come to terms, even before she died, with my mother. When my father actually spoke to me about my mother, he acknowledged that he hadn't taken her two flings as anything other than her tendency not to be able to be committed, or tied down, to anything or anyone.

I understood that, but Mr. Green had broken my heart. He met my eyes as he walked across the waiting area, setting the cat carrier on the counter. I'd learned about the affair from his daughter, an old friend from high school. She lived out of town now. Beyond telling me about it and being furious at her father and my mother, we had never discussed it again. I felt pressed to actually apologize to her, which was ridiculous.

Not that she'd expected it. I'd constantly felt like I had to apologize for the woman my mother was and the mess she left in her wake. Mr. Green dipped his chin, offering, "Hello, Tiffany. I'm here for"—he peered into the cat carrier with a soft smile—"Chester's appointment." His eyes met mine again.

The cat in question, Chester, stared at me through the screened view of the door to his carrier. He looked disgruntled and offended about the situation in which he found himself. I took a deep breath, schooling my expression to neutral, or trying like hell to do so. Chester let out an angry meow.

When I looked back over at Mr. Green, his gaze was steady. "Okay!" I squeaked.

I was ready to cry, but dammit, I wasn't going to burst into tears in front of Mr. Green. I stared at my computer screen and tapped a few keys, barely able to focus. A twisty sense of uncertainty and anxiety slithered through me.

This feeling was unfortunately familiar, and I hated it. It was tied to my mother and would forever be. I associated it solely with her and my younger years when she took me with her as she bounced from job to job. Never knowing what was going to happen didn't feel good. It was also so discombobulating to experience her alternate from treating me with gushing attention to ignoring me when my presence was inconvenient for her.

I'd seen Mr. Green a few times since I had learned of his betrayal. Intellectually, I knew he wasn't the one who had betrayed me. Yet he was... because I looked up to him, I respected him, and I liked him. He'd been my favorite teacher in high school. Chase's too.

"Are you okay?" he asked, his tone steady and warm.

When I looked up at him, I burst into tears. I never looked away, and I sensed he felt helpless and uncertain, wanting to fix the situation yet not even knowing how.

All the while, Chester stared at me as if he somehow realized I was dragging his time out here in the dreaded veterinarian clinic.

Mr. Green's next words made me feel as if he could read my mind. "Tiffany, I'm sorry. I've seen you a few times recently, and you usually avoid me. I know you know what happened. I regret it deeply. I have apologized to Chase and your father, but I haven't had the opportunity to apologize to you. I made a terrible mistake. It hurt my wife, my daughter, and your family."

I snatched a tissue out of the box on the corner of my desk, blowing my nose noisily before looking up at him and shaking my head. "It's not your fault. It's my mother's fault."

The empathy in his eyes almost hurt. Chester meowed. "Your mother was responsible for her actions, of course. But so am I. I regret how this has affected so many people. If I could repair the damage,

I would. I'm simply trying to own it and move forward. A part of that is acknowledging that I'm sure it's affected your respect for me."

The tightness in my chest eased just the tiniest bit. Of course, he had to go and just own it while my mother wasn't here to do that. She'd never owned up to any of her actions and their consequences.

"Thank you," I finally said.

He dipped his chin in acknowledgment. "I wish there was more I could do." He paused, and we both looked at Chester when he let out a wail.

Mr. Green looked back at me, shrugging sheepishly. "Chester is not happy to be here."

"The vet tech will come up to get him," I began as I started to reach to tap the buzzer.

Mr. Green shook his head quickly. "Chester can wait for a minute. I just want to say that I don't know everything about your relationship with your mother. I know it was difficult for you and your brother when you were in high school. Maybe she wasn't the type of person to consider her own actions and the effect they had on others, but she did love you, even if she didn't have the capacity to show it. We are all flawed. Lord knows I'm proof of that. I hope for your own sake that you can find some peace in knowing that you are not her. You are your own person. She was looking for something impossible to find outside one's self. You have it already. You just have to believe it, to believe in your own worth."

This was why Mr. Green had been my favorite teacher in high school. It wasn't that he had deep conversations all the time with students. It was more his steady presence, his centered self, and the way he treated everyone with dignity and respect. Considering how ridiculous high school students could be, that was saying something.

This was why it had been so shocking to discover he'd had a brief fling with my mother. I hadn't thought he would ever be so ridiculous as to fall for her kind of gaudy, effusive flirtatiousness.

"Okay." That was all I could think to say.

"Be kind to yourself. Treat yourself the way you would a good friend. You've always been a good friend."

I swallowed through the tightness in my throat and managed to take a shaky breath. "Okay," I repeated.

Just then, Farrah came through the side door. She glanced at Mr. Green and me. "Oh, is that Chester?" she asked, gesturing to Chester, who let out an operatic wail as he looked over at her.

Her eyes landed on mine. It was obvious I'd been crying. But Mr. Green was here, so her worried eyes shifted from me to him.

I gathered myself quickly, saying, "This is Chester. And Mr. Green, my favorite high school teacher." My chirpy voice was almost too bright.

Farrah smiled at him before shooting another glance at me. "Are you ready to go in the back?" she finally asked.

Mr. Green nodded. "Whenever you are. Chester is known for playing dead once we get in there."

Farrah snorted a laugh, and I couldn't help but giggle. "Well, that's a change of pace," she mused as she lifted the cat carrier. They walked to the back together.

———

Hours later, the workday had ended. The last patient, a silly rabbit who had escaped and bounced down the hallway after her appointment, had left with her owner. I was cleaning up the waiting area where a nervous dog had peed in three locations.

The door to the back opened, and Farrah peered in. "Oh, there you are." Her eyes dropped to where I was cleaning. "Who did that?"

"The puppy," I said with a shrug. "It's expected."

I straightened after I finished wiping the area with the disinfectant spray that broke down the scent. "The cleaning people will come tonight and give it another cleaning," I noted as I crossed to the trashcan and tied it up after tossing in the wipes.

I double-checked that the entrance door was locked and my computer was powered down before walking with Farrah to the back.

"Are you okay?" she asked as we walked into the break room together.

I shrugged as I looked over at her. "I think so. You caught me at a bad moment earlier."

"What happened?" Alice asked as she walked in, clearly hearing my reply.

Looking between them, I hesitated for a beat before Alice prompted, "Let me know if I can do anything."

I took a breath before I sat down at the table and rested my hands on my face for a moment. Straightening, I tightened my ponytail before letting my hands fall. "It's a whole thing. I haven't talked about it, but I put a pause on things with Wes and me." I glanced at Farrah before looking at Alice. "You know how my mom was, right?"

Alice and Farrah immediately sat at the table.

Farrah offered, "I don't know how your mom was, but this calls for friend time. What do you need?"

My eyes felt watery. "I'm not sure where to start."

"I sensed there was a pause with you and Wes, but since you weren't talking about it, I didn't want to push," Alice said. "And what does this have to do with your mom? As far as what I knew about your mom, all I knew was she wasn't around a lot. When you were younger, she used to take you with her. Sometime in middle school, it seemed like that stopped happening." She glanced at Farrah. "Small town. Tiffany and I were friends but not besties in school. Kids notice when kids aren't around all the time, though."

"Where is your mom now?" Farrah asked the obvious question.

"She died," I said simply.

"Oh! I'm sorry!" Farrah looked dismayed.

"Thank you. It's been a few years. I had a complicated relationship with her. She was kind of, well, not really the most available mom. She did a number on both Chase and me. When I was younger, I was her favorite but not in a healthy way. Not that there's any healthy way to have a favorite, but she took me with her everywhere while traipsing around trying to get famous. She wanted to be a model, she wanted to be an actress, she wanted to be in a band, and so on. She was desperate for attention, so she was always taking new jobs here and there. It finally stopped when she had her first of two affairs. I was really stressed out. I was getting behind in school, so my dad put his foot down. My dad is really good about not saying anything bad about her. He was then, and he still is now, but he was willing to argue with her about me staying in place. She ran hot and cold, so it was just a mess." I lifted a hand, waving it vaguely and hesitating. "I don't know if I want to say this because it might affect what you think of Mr. Green."

"Mr. Green made you cry," Farrah said pointedly. "I didn't go to high school here, so I'm not attached to him."

Alice shrugged. "Let me guess, he had an affair with your mom."

"Did you already know that?" I sucked my breath in through my teeth as I gave her a dismayed look.

"Small town. There were rumors," she said succinctly.

I let out a weary sigh. "They were true. It was just a weekend. His daughter, Frannie, told me. He and his wife are trying to work things out. It happened a few months before my mom died. Even though I was furious with him..." I paused, almost doing a physical scan of my body.

I wasn't mad at him anymore. Somehow, that brief interaction with him had helped me to let it go, to recognize that even though he had let me down, he was just a flawed person, like the whole wide world. "I was mad, but I'm not now," I finally said. "He apologized. My mom can never apologize, though she probably wouldn't have." I twisted my fingers in my lap as I looked at my two friends. "She wasn't the kind of person to contemplate her behavior in the context of how it affected others. Long story short, I don't have a great track record with trust in relationships. I was angry with her after she died because my dad is the best. He deserved a good relationship, someone to treat him right. So..." I threw a hand up in the air before letting it fall. "I haven't even talked about it, but I have this thing on my back, a peripheral nerve sheath tumor." I rolled my eyes. "This guy I started to see, I actually trusted him, and he just ghosted me completely when I had the thing with my back."

Farrah interjected. "Are you okay?"

Alice answered for me. "She had surgery, and she's fine."

Farrah let out a breath. "Okay, I just needed to know that. Carry on."

"And then this whole thing happened with Wes. We've got Ross, and it just seems like it's..." I ran out of words and leaned back in my chair, exhausted from trying to explain.

"Like it's too much of a risk," Farrah said calmly.

When I met her eyes, I realized she completely understood.

"I get it. It's logical, emotionally speaking. Except Wes is really into you," she added.

Alice nodded vigorously. "He is. No wonder he looked so down when I saw him. You know the crew is going out for three weeks starting tomorrow."

"I know," I said quickly. Until this very moment, I'd thought that was a good thing. It would give me some space where I didn't have to worry about running into him in town and be so concerned about constantly wanting to call and text him because I wouldn't be able to. But now, I felt a sense of panic. I needed to reach out and grab him to make sure everything was okay. I beat back that feeling. "Yeah, I know. Ross is coming over tomorrow. He'll be with me while Wes is gone. That's why this whole shared guardianship has to work out. We have to put Ross first."

Alice gave me a quizzical look. "Okay, sure, but..." She pressed her lips together, narrowing her eyes as she studied me. "I think Wes means more to you than you're willing to admit. I wouldn't be your friend if I didn't point out that you're breaking your own heart, along with his."

I looked toward Farrah as if she would dispute Alice's point. She shrugged, her lips twisting to the side. "She has a point."

Chapter Thirty-Eight

TIFFANY

Wes had been gone for a full week. I missed him every single day and night. It wasn't as if we'd been spending every night together before I put a pause on things, but we had been texting and communicating regularly. The simple fact that I couldn't do that left a hollow ache inside my chest.

Ross and I settled into a routine. The more time I spent with him, the more my heart felt split open. I missed Sarah. Maybe it had been a few years since we'd been in the same place and getting together for coffee or dinner, but the permanence of her absence felt huge. When we were college roommates, our lives had been twined together. I missed being able to text her quick jokes and observations about my day.

I was still shocked at her death and felt like the universe had been brutally unfair. Ross had spoken of his parents a few more times and even cried one night when a show his mom had liked came on. When I said I didn't have to watch it, he asked me to do it anyway because it made him think of her. He said it made him feel safe.

One evening, I came home from work feeling ragged along the edges. Alice had to send someone's dog over the rainbow bridge. Even though there was still snow on the ground, we'd done it outside because the family said he'd loved the snow.

The dog hadn't eaten for a full week. He was weak and tired and suffering from kidney and liver failure. He was also fifteen years old, a long life for any dog. Watching the love this family had for their dog and their choice to put him out of his discomfort was a gift, I thought. It was also heartbreaking.

I picked up Ross and Nilla from my dad's, where they'd spent the afternoon. Nilla had spent the day with my dad, and Ross took the bus there after school.

Ross had glanced over in the car, studying me for a moment before he asked, "Are you crying about missing Wes?"

The wisdom of children. I glanced at him before another tear slid down my cheek as I tried to shake my head.

Ross cocked his head to the side, looking quizzical. "You miss him. I do too. I can't even play my game with him and Chase at night right now. It's weird because my dad's username is still in there, and I miss him too."

I swallowed a sob and blinked quickly, my hands tightening on the steering wheel as I looked ahead. "I do miss Wes. I'm so sorry about your mom and dad. I'm sure you miss them a lot."

I glanced sideways, wondering if I should pull over. Ross was looking out the window. We happened to be driving by a field where several moose were gathered off to the side.

"You don't have to say you're sorry. It's not your fault," Ross said quietly without looking my way.

I looked back at the road, replying, "I'm sorry that it happened, sorry that life is unfair like that."

"It is," he said simply. "How come you made Wes sad?"

I whipped my head to the side to find Ross looking back at me again. I blinked again, bringing my attention to the road. There was a viewing area on the road ahead. I pulled off and parked. A guardrail was situated above a rocky ledge that looked out into a valley with a glacier in the distance and the mountains rising high around it.

I angled in my seat to face Ross. "Why do you think I made Wes sad?" I asked as my heart pounded rapidly in my chest.

"I haven't heard him cry like you did the other night," he began.

I *had* cried the other night in my bedroom, missing Wes and missing Sarah.

"But you haven't kissed him again, and he looks sad when you call."

I was determined not to cry and took a deep breath, steadying myself as I scrambled to try to think of how to reply to this.

"I think you like him a lot," Ross added.

I scrunched my nose and then let out a soft sigh. "I do like Wes. A lot."

"You're worried something might mess things up, and you want to make sure I'm okay. I'm okay." He reached over and patted my hand where it rested on the console.

Staring at this little boy, I wondered how he could have so much wisdom and be so young. "I know you're okay. I promise Wes and I will figure things out, but we're here for you. You're our priority."

"I know," he said simply.

———

The following day, Farrah stood beside my desk, arms akimbo, as she eyed me. "You're cranky," she announced. "You miss Wes. Why don't you just admit you really love him?"

"Farrah!" I sputtered.

She shrugged. "I get it. You've got baggage. Welcome to life. We all do. It's that whole bag of rocks thing we're all carrying. Some of those rocks are pretty jagged. I get your thing with your mom and that stupid guy who ghosted you. You have two choices: carry that weight forever or toss those rocks out. We could even do some kind of woo-woo ceremony, where we get you a rock, and you throw it," she offered.

Alice happened to appear in the doorway just then and burst out laughing. She divided a look between us. "I'm all in on the throwing the rock ceremony. Where shall we go for this? Maybe we go down to my place and do it off the dock."

Farrah grinned, her hands falling from her hips. "Perfect."

Just then, Alice's cell phone chimed, and she slipped it out of her pocket, glancing down. Her brows hitched up as she looked back at us. "It's the hospital. That's weird." She slid her thumb across the screen. "Hello?"

The moment she answered the call, an unnerving sense of anxiety, bordering on panic, began to spin inside of my chest. I felt a little sick. I wanted to snatch the phone from her and demand answers. I didn't know what was happening, but everything in my body told me something had happened to Wes.

"Uh-huh, okay. She's right here." Alice handed me
her phone.

Chapter Thirty-Nine

WES

Five hours earlier

Even though I was breathing cool spring air and patches of snow were still on the ground, the flames cast off walls of heat. I heard the sound of a helicopter above, glancing up to see it angling to the side before dropping water. It had been a dry winter for this area of the state, like much of the west in general. The fire had been set off by sparks from a faulty electrical line in one of the small villages nearby. Fortunately for the village, the wind had driven it away, but we needed to establish a perimeter and get the fire out before it changed direction again.

I turned my attention back to what I was doing, steadily working with the chainsaw, creating a perimeter along the edge of a river. Fortunately, that hadn't dried up yet. I was tired, but I kept on moving, as we all did. I wouldn't have been able to tell you exactly what happened. All I knew was the blade of my chainsaw hit an unexpected rock, and it kicked back. By the grace of fucking God, the chainsaw missed me, but I stumbled against a tree that was still smoking from the fire that had burned through the area only hours before we got to this section. I cried out abruptly as I fell.

I was conscious when the guy working closest to me, Chase, reached me. My vision was blurry as I looked up at him. "Please tell me my side looks okay."

Chase's eyes were worried as he looked at me. "Okay is relative. We've gotta get you out of here."

God only knew why I chose then to blurt this out, but I did. "I love Tiffany," I said between ragged breaths.

Chase had already opened a backpack that appeared out of nowhere, it seemed. Rowan arrived, and they both began peeling my clothing away to check the burn on my side.

Chase looked at me, replying, "I don't think now is the best time for this conversation, but I already knew that. You're a dumbass."

"Why is he a dumbass?" Rowan asked.

My breath hissed through my teeth as I felt him carefully peeling away my shirt from the area where I'd collided with the smoldering tree. Chase glanced at Rowan as they continued working. "It doesn't look too bad, maybe a second-degree burn. It's gonna leave a nasty scar. I think we just clean the area and cover it up for now. He's a dumbass because he decided to tell me he loves my sister. Now."

Rowan let out a chuckle. "A little pain will do that." His eyes met mine. "Hang on, we're going to spray that antiseptic, numbing stuff on this. It'll burn for a sec."

"Can't be worse than—" I let out to get another

sharp breath as I felt a stinging spray on my side, the sensation immediately followed by numbing.

"You've been moping around for weeks," Rowan said as he efficiently placed a bandage over the area. "We all know you're in love with Tiffany. Why don't you do something about it?"

A while later, after they had walked me over to an area where a helicopter could land and lift me, Chase was waiting beside me.

He glanced over. "I don't know how much Tiffany told you, but our mom was a hot mess. Trust is hard for her. Just know that. If you love her, you might have to go out of your way to help her believe she can trust you. And if you ever fuck her over, I will make your life fucking miserable." His tone was gruff.

"Understood. Is there something specific I should know about your mom?"

He shrugged, looking away. "She was never really around. And when Tiffany was younger, she dragged her around with her. It was hard. She had two affairs." He looked back at me. "We both hated her for it because our dad was rock solid and deserved better."

———

What felt like hours later, they wheeled me into the hospital in a wheelchair. I had resisted, but Graham insisted it was necessary.

Once I was there, it felt like I had entered a time warp. The hospital was a *process*, and you had to abandon all control once you were there. The emergency room was busy. I could hear a jumble of noise around me before a doctor arrived, announcing, "We're taking you into the OR. We need to clean the burn wound."

The last thing I recalled was Holly Blake coming in to check on me. Beyond growing up in Willow Brook together, Holly's husband was the very guy who'd flown me out in a helicopter after the injury. Her concerned blue eyes held mine. "Wes, you're going to be fine. I promise."

"I need you to do me a favor." Whatever medication they had just given me was making me a little woozy, but my brain was focused on two people: Ross and Tiffany. "Call Tiffany and let her know what happened. Make sure she and Ross know I'll be okay. Tell her I love her."

Chapter Forty

TIFFANY

"Who?" I said into my phone.

"Holly."

"Oh, hey, Holly. How are you?"

I was a little confused by Holly calling me. Of course, we were friends. Holly was friends with pretty much everybody around our age in town.

"I'm at the hospital. I'm calling about Wes. Before I say anything else, he's going to be fine."

The moment she said Wes's name, my stomach plummeted. I felt as if I was in an elevator shaft dropping dramatically at an unexpected speed.

Holly was an ER nurse, and she was calling about Wes. That had to mean Wes was at the hospital.

"What happened?" I barked into the phone.

"A burn. Honestly, it looks ugly, but he's in surgery so the doctor can clean it up. If it weren't for the debris in the wound, he probably wouldn't need surgery. He asked me to call you and let you and Ross know he would be okay."

It felt as if my heart had stumbled and was racing downhill. Each beat felt reckless and out of control. I tried to take a calming breath, but it did nothing to slow my heartbeat or quell the anxiety rising swiftly inside.

"What happened? When did he go into surgery? How long is he going to be in there? And how do you know he's actually going to be okay? Things can happen with anesthesia."

Holly's tone was soothing. "I don't know exactly what happened. All I know is that he fell and collided with a charred tree that was still smoldering from the fire. The burn is on his side. Why don't you come down to the hospital so you can be here when he gets out of surgery? You'll tell Ross that he's going to be okay?" she prompted.

"Of course, of course," I said quickly. "I'll come to the hospital."

I looked around my office, relieved it was close to the end of the day. Ross was at my father's this afternoon, so I'd need to call over there. Thoughts bounced around my brain like a pinball game.

"One more thing," Holly said.

"What's that?"

"Wes said to tell you that he loves you."

I had no idea if I even said anything else. A moment later, Alice found me sitting in the chair at my desk on the verge of hyperventilating. I felt her palm land between my shoulder blades.

"Lean over, rest your elbows on your knees, and breathe," she said, her tone perfectly calm even though she didn't know what was happening.

I did as she instructed, listening to my breath as it gradually slowed. I didn't know how much time had passed, but the tingly feeling that had radiated throughout my body started to recede, and I felt like I could get air into my lungs.

"I think you can sit up now."

I slowly straightened, not even realizing I'd been crying until Alice reached for the box of tissues on my desk and handed me one. "What happened?" she asked.

"Wes got hurt. He's at the hospital. Holly said he got burned by a tree, and he's going into surgery to clean the wound."

Alice's eyes widened, but she stayed calm, unlike me. "So he'll be okay?"

"She said so, but—"

Alice's palm pressed firmly between my shoulder blades. "Don't go there. Don't make trouble where there isn't. Let's get you to the hospital."

"But—" I glanced wildly around the waiting area to see absolutely no one there.

"I just had my last appointment. We walked out together, and they left," Alice explained. "I'll have Farrah lock up and drive you to the hospital."

"I can drive," I protested. I hated needing anyone.

Alice didn't even address my comment. She called over her shoulder to Farrah, who had just appeared at the doorway from the back hallway. "Go get her keys."

That snapped through the static of panic in my brain, and I stared at her before letting out an offended huff. "Okay, fine. I probably shouldn't drive. But if you're going to drive, we have to go get Ross. He's at my dad's house."

"I'll call your dad. He can meet us at the hospital."

"But—" I began, only to have Farrah cut me off.

"You're in no shape to keep Ross calm. Your dad is as steady as a rock. He'll meet us there. That way, Ross can get the update. Maybe he should spend the night with your dad."

I looked back and forth between my two friends.

Even though I wanted to argue the point, I knew they were both right. I took a shaky breath as I nodded. Looking over at Farrah, I added, "You don't have to take my keys."

"I'll drive you to the hospital. Farrah can drop your car off at the hospital after she closes up. After I get you to the hospital, we'll ask Maisie to pick her up and bring her back. That way, your car is exactly where it needs to be. Sound like a plan?" Alice prompted.

As I looked at them, I burst into tears. Back when I'd been in Seattle and gotten sick and my boyfriend/asshole friend had blown me off, I'd felt so alone. Now, I felt completely supported.

"We've got you," Farrah said.

I gave them a watery smile as I nodded before taking another tissue and blowing my nose.

Chapter Forty-One

TIFFANY

Time passed in increments as I waited at the hospital. My father had come and gone with Ross. Holly had agreed to text him as soon as Wes came out of surgery, so my dad would bring Ross back. My dad was taking Ross for pizza and assured me a distraction was best. I agreed, but I was still a mess. Alice was with me, and Farrah had somehow magically already brought my car to the hospital and given me my keys. Maisie had stopped by to give me a hug.

Wes's mom had arrived, pulling me aside. Her eyes, so like his, held mine as she clasped my hands. "Wes loves you. I hope you'll give him a chance."

That was it. That was all she said. She didn't press for explanations from me or chastise me for maybe hurting his feelings while I tried to get my shit together. She offered pure acceptance.

I swallowed through the thickness in my throat, nodding as I blinked back my tears. "I love him too," I said, my voice a ragged whisper.

Alice was sitting beside me while I blindly flipped

through a magazine. "How are you doing?" she asked, her tone soft.

I glanced at her closing the magazine and setting it on the table beside me before twisting my fingers together. "Not so great."

"Maybe you could consider what your feelings for Wes mean."

"Now?"

Alice cocked her head to the side, her gaze understanding and more perceptive than I wished. "Maybe I'm an idiot, but I'm pretty sure you're in love with him. Life is complicated all the time. I know you both have Ross to consider, but in a way, I think that means you'll take it more seriously. I know it's a different situation, but that's what I think about with Jonah's grandmother. It would've been messy if she really wanted us to work out, and we tried to make it work, and it didn't. But it would've been okay. You and Wes falling in love, well, it could be really good. Important issues, in my opinion, make us think more seriously about what we do and our choices about how we treat each other."

I swallowed, staring at her as my heart kicked along in my chest. I knew she was right. I also knew that this event had only illuminated the size of my love for Wes. It was big, encompassing so much space in my heart. The idea of letting it slip away felt like I was giving up on the most real thing I'd ever experienced with someone.

At that moment, Holly came striding briskly into the waiting area. Her blond hair was pulled up in a ponytail that swung as she glanced around the room. Her eyes landed on me. "He's out of surgery and in recovery," she announced.

"When can I see him?"

Holly stopped in front of me, replying, "In just a few minutes. He can only see one person at a time."

Wes's mother, Jane, glanced over at me. "You're going first," she announced.

"Are you sure you don't want to see him first?"

She smiled warmly. "Wes loves you. Pretty sure he loves me too, but I can wait. All I need to know is that he's okay."

"Everything went okay in surgery?" Alice asked, ever practical.

"It went well. He's going to be sore and have a nice scar, but he'll be fine. We got him all cleaned up too," Holly assured us.

"Is there anything we need to worry about for recovery? And when will he be out?" I asked.

"He can be discharged as soon as they clear him in recovery. Usually, that takes..." Holly moved her hand back and forth. "About two hours. We need to make sure his pain is managed. Let me go check on him, and then I'll come get you. Should be just a few minutes."

I was way too nervous and couldn't sit down after that. I paced in a loop in the waiting area with my arms crossed tightly. It felt like forever—even though the clock told me it was only a few minutes—by the time Holly reappeared, beckoning me with her hand. "Follow me."

After a short walk down a hallway, she stopped in front of a door and glanced over her shoulder. "Other people are in the recovery area, but there's a sliding door, so you'll have privacy." Her eyes were twinkling. "He's a little loopy."

A moment later, I was alone in the room with Wes. I heard the door slide closed behind me. Wes was lying in bed wearing a hospital gown with the blankets tucked around his hips. He still had an IV in. Just looking at him made my heart ache. He didn't usually look vulnerable, but here, he did. His dark hair contrasted with the white pillows he was propped on. He rolled his head to the side, and a slow smile broke across his face when he saw me.

"Hey," he said slowly. "You're here."

Tears spilled over my cheeks as I crossed the small room to his side and rested my hands on the bed railing. My throat ached, and my chest felt tight. "Of course I'm here," I croaked.

"Did you get my message?"

I blinked away my tears before dragging my sleeve across my face. "Ross will be here soon. My dad took him to get pizza until you were out."

"Oh man, I'd love some pizza," he said, his voice a little slow.

"I love you!" I burst out as more tears rolled down my cheeks.

Wes looked at me, reaching for my hand, his touch a little clumsy. He missed, but I caught his hand. It was the hand with the IV needle taped on the back of it. I carefully adjusted the IV line so it didn't get tangled in the bed railing.

"That was my other message," he said. "Really important stuff. Why are you crying?"

I sniffled and shrugged, my lips tugging into a smile. "It is really important stuff."

He squeezed my hand, his eyes holding mine. "I know you're worried about it being complicated, but it'll be okay. I'm not going to fall out of love with you."

I leaned over and pressed a kiss to his cheek. "I love you too. I want to give us a chance. I'm not planning on falling out of love with you, either. I suppose it's complicated no matter what."

"Oh, thank God!" he exclaimed. "I thought I was going to have to really persuade you."

I smiled down at him, brushing his hair back. "I missed you," I whispered hoarsely.

"I missed you too." He never looked away as his eyes held mine. "We're going to be okay."

"We are?"

Even though he'd just come out of surgery to clean a burn wound, he smiled. I could've sworn I saw the banked embers of desire flickering in his eyes. "Yeah. I love you. You love me. We have a lot of reasons to make it work."

My heart felt as if a light was flooding into it after too many days of darkness. The curtains pushed back, and the windows flung open with a fresh spring breeze gusting through. I thought about what Alice had said. Despite my worries about Ross and the complications that came with Wes and me being his guardians, his presence would push us to take it seriously. That meant we would be more fair to each other, stay on the field of honesty, and have the difficult conversations.

I felt the brush of Wes's thumb on the inside of my palm, and I took a deep breath, steadying myself. "I love you," I repeated. "I'm sorry—"

He shook his head. "There's nothing to apologize for. You needed some space. I think it's obvious neither one of us planned on this. None of it." His voice became gruff. "I was terrified."

"Of what?"

"That I'd gone and fallen in love with someone who didn't love me back. You're it for me, Tiffany," he said solemnly.

The craziest thing of all was I believed him. All this time, I'd felt like something was inherently wrong with me. I'd carried my mother's baggage when it wasn't even mine to carry. I'd held on to secrets that weren't mine to keep and the painful lessons my mother never quite learned. Or if she did, I couldn't tell.

"Promise me you'll always be a little prickly, but with that heart of gold who loves everyone," he said.

"If I loved everyone, didn't that mean automatically I would love you?" I teased.

Wes chuckled. "You know what I mean. You give everyone a chance but yourself. I *see* you, Tiffany, and I love you just the way you are."

My throat felt tight, and I swallowed through the thickness.

Just then, I heard the distinct slide of the door and the curtain being pushed back as Holly called out, "Are we decent?"

A startled laugh sputtered out of me. "I'm decent," he teased in return as Holly peered around the curtain.

She waggled her eyebrows as she stepped into the room. "Just checking. Ross and your mom are waiting to come in."

"Should I go out front?" I asked.

Holly slid me a look and put a finger to her lips. "Just stand in the corner and stay quiet."

I pressed my lips together to keep from laughing as I nodded.

Ross and Wes's mom came in. His mom fussed over him a bit. When I saw the worried look in Ross's eyes, I almost started crying. Yet he was so happy Wes was okay. He chattered nonstop for a few minutes, updating Wes on my dad, how Nilla was doing, and how he would make sure to be quiet when they played video games during Wes's recovery.

Just before they were about to leave, his mom

glanced over. "I've already talked to your dad, and Ross is going to stay with him tonight. Then he'll come to my place for the next two nights. We've got the whole thing lined out, food and everything."

"Nilla can go everywhere too," Ross said with a big smile.

Holly was coming back in as they left. She checked a few things on the monitor and then glanced between Wes and me. "He can discharge in about a half hour. We need to make sure you feel okay sitting up. All signs look good. How are you feeling?"

"Ready to leave," he said.

A short while later, I was driving, feeling unaccountably nervous. I felt like I was carrying precious cargo. Yet Wes was a grown-ass man. My God, he was a hotshot firefighter.

Perhaps what felt fragile was my heart and the depth of my feelings. Wes had looked straight into my eyes. I'd felt that he could see me just as I was—a little messy, not so trusting with romance, and maybe kinda pushy too. He loved me anyway.

Chapter Forty-Two

WES

Tiffany had wanted to stop by her place, but Alice and Farrah, my two favorite people in the universe tonight, had refused to let her do that. Farrah had even threatened to take her keys away. They were going to go to her place and get her a bag and her things. We had to go up the stairs to get to her place, whereas I only had to climb three stairs to get inside mine. Even though I was pretty sure I was fine, I could feel the threatening ache under the anesthesia and numbing starting to fade on my side.

Roughly an hour or so later, after Alice and Farrah had delivered a bag for Tiffany with clothes and toiletries for the next few days and done a quick run to the grocery store and brought some food for us, it was just Tiffany and me. She was nervous. She flitted about my place, putting away the groceries, and asking me if I wanted some soup. Even though I knew I was going to be hungry later, I wasn't right now.

She put the backpack in the hallway by my bedroom door, inexplicably not carrying it in. She had me situated on the couch with my legs propped up on the cushioned ottoman and a blanket draped over my waist. "Tiffany," I finally said.

She was in the kitchen making tea for me even though I didn't give a flying fuck about tea. She turned, mug in hand. "I'm coming."

She hurried over, setting the mug on the coffee table beside the couch. She fussed over me, adjusting the blanket on my lap and checking to make sure I had enough pillows behind me. She'd collected every loose pillow on the couch and piled them around me. I felt like she would've wrapped me in bubble wrap if it was possible.

I shoved the pillows over, patting the couch beside me. "Sit, please."

She sat down, her worried eyes coasting over my face. I took a moment to study her. She had her hair pulled up in a messy bun with a pen stuck through it to hold it in place. Dark locks had fallen loose around her neck. I wanted to kiss every freckle scattered on her cheeks.

"Thank you for the tea," I said, genuinely grateful she was fussing over me even if I didn't care about the tea itself.

She laced her fingers together, her thumb rubbing over a silver ring on one of her fingers. I reached for one of her hands, and she didn't hesitate, unlacing her fingers and curling her palm around mine.

"You're worried," I said.

She looked at me like I was insane. "Of course I'm worried!" she burst out. "You were out doing your hotshot firefighter thing and got hurt. You had to have surgery."

"I'm fine," I insisted, gesturing up and down my body. "See. Good as new. Just going to have a scar from my trouble." I waggled my brows. "I hear scars are sexy."

Tiffany cocked her head to the side, a smile teasing at the corners of her lips. "It'll be sexy when I'm not afraid you might die."

I was about to tease her in return when a tear rolled down her cheek. "Hey, hey," I murmured, shifting so I could pull her closer to my side. "I was never at any risk of dying," I assured her as I curled an arm around her back, sliding my palm up and down in soothing passes.

She curled into me, tucking her head into the curve of my shoulder. Her fingertips traced the collar of my T-shirt. "You don't know that." Her tone was watery, and she sniffled.

"Tiffany, look at me."

She shifted, straightening and looking into my eyes. My hand slid from her back, and I lifted it to palm her cheek, wiping one of her tears with my thumb. "Maybe not, but what matters is I'm fine now."

She blinked before nodding. I shifted again, levering her closer and bringing my mouth to hers. I meant for it to be a brief kiss, a comforting kiss. But I'd been out fighting a fire in the wilderness for two weeks. Before that, I hadn't kissed her in too long, *way* too long.

She drew back, just barely. We studied each other. My heart was like a thundering drumroll through my body, heralding my love for her, my need for her, my fierce and simple want for her.

Chapter Forty-Three

TIFFANY

Wes was intent. His gaze roamed over me. "Come here," he murmured, catching my hand in his as he stood, tugging me with him.

I stepped closer, asking, "Are you okay?"

"Of course." He dipped his head, bringing his lips to mine.

Our kiss started slow but quickly spiraled into hot and intense. His tongue swept into my mouth, his hands sliding into my hair as he angled my head to the side, taking command.

A moment later, we broke apart, gasping together.

"I need you," he rasped.

"Wes," I tried to protest, thinking he was in no shape for sex.

"I missed you. I need you."

He nudged me back into the bedroom. It was a blur as he tugged at my clothes. I realized we both needed this. His hands mapped me before he stretched me out on the bed. I was mindful of his side, where the bandaging was.

Everything felt rushed but also suspended in time

as if we were caught in a net of shimmering sparks with our need binding us together. Every beat of my heart was an echoing drumroll through my body.

His mouth was hot on mine, the brush of his stubble against my skin sending sparks in a fiery shimmer through me. His weight came down over me, and I felt the thick press of his crown at my entrance before he filled me. He brushed my hair back from my face, resting on his elbows as he stared into my eyes. I felt stripped raw as if my heart had been cleaved open.

"Wes," I whispered.

WES

At the sound of my name, I thrust forward, filling Tiffany in one deep surge. Her eyes fell closed, and she let out a shuddery breath. I held still, savoring the feel of her slick channel pulsing around me.

When her eyes opened again, I whispered, "I love you."

"Love—you —Wes—" She gasped between ragged breaths as I rocked into her.

This between us was pure, elemental. It was sex, but it was so much more. I had missed her so fiercely that I hadn't even let myself feel the depth of it until she was with me again.

Moments later, I felt her tightening and shuddering. I shifted the angle of my hips, reaching between us to tease my fingers over her very core, just where she needed it. She came, sobbing my name as she clenched around me.

I followed her over the edge, emotion rushing through me like a waterfall tumbling over a mountainside. I rolled to my good side, and she followed, curling against me.

Afterward, I simply held her, savoring her against me and all we had together. Several minutes passed before she lifted her head. Her gaze held mine as she studied me.

"We have to get this right," she said.

"We will. We'll do whatever it takes."

EPILOGUE
Tiffany

Six months later

Chase stared at me. His hand was curled around the top of a dolly, which was stacked with boxes. My brother looked back at me, replying, "Oh, we're finishing today. You're just panicking."

"I'm not panicking!" I protested. "It's almost eight o'clock. And—"

My sister-in-law appeared in the doorway. "I'm here with a baby who is sound asleep. If I can keep going, we all can. Also, Alice, Farrah, and Maisie are bringing pizza to Wes's place in a half hour. I'm just the messenger. Let Chase help finish loading this last bit. Alice says you and her and Farrah are cleaning the apartment tomorrow."

I looked from my brother to Hallie and let out a little laugh. My heart felt full. I had family and friends and Wes. The love in my life felt big, too big for my heart almost. There was the family that you had and the family you made. Mine felt like it kept getting bigger every year.

Speaking of, my declared sister McKenna appeared in the doorway, tightening the ponytail on top of her head. "Last set of boxes," she announced.

———

That night, Ross looked around the living room as Nilla studiously continued to sniff every new box that had been brought into the house. Ross smiled up at me. "Wow, you have a lot of stuff."

Resting my hands on my hips, I rolled my eyes. "Not really. It's just moving is the house equivalent of vomiting."

Ross's brows flew up. "Ew. That's a weird way to describe it. I mean, it makes sense, though," he added.

Wes chuckled as he appeared at the end of the short hallway that led to the bedrooms. "It is. I'm starving."

As if on cue, McKenna came walking through the front door with several boxes of pizza in her arms. "Hi, I'm your mind reader," she announced with a grin.

We settled in to eat pizza together, with Alice and Farrah arriving after declaring earlier they were going to clean my apartment tonight so I didn't have to go back tomorrow. They'd passed on the pizza pickup to McKenna. I had wanted to argue the point, but I was exhausted. Because moving was tiring.

After I finished my last slice of pizza, I leaned back into the cushions on the couch, looking around at my friends. Alice was laughing at something McKenna said while Chase had already gotten up to help Wes relocate a dresser from my place into Wes's bedroom.

Wes was already going to have to re-organize the closet and add some shelving and more rods for clothes. He had assured me he would have it taken care of within the week. Not that I was fussing about it.

I was still a little shocked this was happening, almost feeling fragile about it. It might blow away with a gust of wind if I thought too long about the reality of it.

Farrah was seated beside me on the couch. When my eyes made their way to her, she smiled. "You did the hard thing," she said softly.

"I did?"

She angled her head to the side, her eyes knowing. "Absolutely. I don't think falling in love is easy. And like everyone, you had to jump through an obstacle course in your own mind to get here."

I snorted at that. "I suppose so." My eyes landed on Ross. "I just hope it's okay for Ross."

"He'll be okay. He's been through more than any boy should with his parents dying, but he's got both of you and…" Pausing, she gestured around the room. "Everyone here. I'm a firm believer that unfair things do happen, but the universe is usually generous in other ways. Everyone here would go to bat for that kid."

My throat tightened, and I took a breath. My heart felt full to bursting at moments.

I watched as her eyes arced about the room, landing on Hayes, one of the newer firefighters on Wes and Chase's crew. Many of them had been by to help with the move as the day had carried on. Only a few were left. Hayes was another local who'd returned to the nest of Willow Brook. He and Wes had been good friends in high school.

I cleared my throat, and Farrah's eyes whipped back to mine. I waggled my brows. "Hayes, huh?"

She narrowed her eyes. "I'm just enjoying the view."

I looked over at Hayes. He had rumpled, almost black curls paired with deep green eyes. And, of course, he was a hotshot firefighter, so he was seriously fit. I glanced back over at Farrah again. "Considering that he would look great in a firefighter calendar, he gives a good view, but you don't look at anybody else like that."

She tended to be unflappable, but her cheeks tinged pink. I nudged her with my elbow, teasing, "You can have the hots for Hayes."

"Shut up," she grumbled.

The following morning, we went for coffee and brunch at Firehouse Café. Janet arrived at our table, resting her hand on Ross's shoulder and squeezing gently. "Good morning. What would you like for breakfast?"

She flipped her braid on her shoulder as he peered up at her. "You know my favorite."

"Biscuits and gravy?" she prompted.

"Extra gravy," he replied with a grin.

Her gaze arced from Wes to me. "And you two?"

"I'll take the same," Wes chimed in.

I added, "Same."

I took a swallow of my coffee.

"That makes it easy," Janet replied. "You're all moved in?"

"Well, everything is moved, but now I have to organize it."

"At least it's all in one place." She glanced at her watch. "Your food will be out in about fifteen minutes." She glanced over her shoulder at the line, her gaze arcing around the busy café and back to us. "Usually, it's quicker, but we're busy."

"No worries," Wes offered. "We like it here."

Janet smiled at him. "You ready for fire season?"

"I'd better be because I'll be heading out soon."

"Now you've got Tiffany to hold down the fort at home."

"And me," Ross chimed in.

She ruffled his hair and hurried off. Wes squeezed my knee under the table as Ross lifted his phone and started playing a game on it. When my eyes lifted to his, Wes mouthed, "I love you."

I leaned over and dropped a kiss on his shoulder. Ross happened to look up just then and rolled his eyes.

A little while later, Wes was driving, and Ross was in the back with Nilla, who had gotten one of Janet's dog biscuits for breakfast. We were headed to the beach for a walk.

I still can't believe this is my life sometimes. I didn't realize I'd said that out loud.

Wes reached across the console, lacing his fingers through mine and squeezing. "Believe it."

Thank you for reading Wes & Tiffany's story! Want a glimpse of the future for them? Join my newsletter to receive an exclusive scene.

Sign up here: https://BookHip.com/DZDNLVQ

p.s. If you are already subscribed, you'll still be able to access the scene.

My next release kicks off the Fireweed Harbor Series - a new small town series set in Alaska. Make You Mine is Rhys & Haven's second chance romance.

Rhys is practically royalty in Fireweed Harbor, the wealthy CEO of his family's corporation. He's devilishly handsome, broody and best friends with Haven's older brother. He barely noticed her back in high school.

Sparks fly when they meet again. What starts as a fun fling turns into much more. Until a blast from the past upends everything. Haven vows never to give him another chance.

You know what they say about never? Buckle up for one hot, hot, hot second chance romance when Rhys fights to win Haven back!

Pre-order Make You Mine - due out April 11, 2023!

Up next in the Light My Fire Series is Take Me Now.

Farrah & Cooper are neighbors who don't believe in love. When the chemistry between them is enough to light up the sky, they figure friends with benefits will be enough.

Until it isn't.

Don't miss Farrah & Cooper's story - it's swoony, emotional & sweet!

Pre-order Take Me Now - due out August 15, 2023!

For more swoony romance...

This Crazy Love kicks off the Swoon Series - small town southern romance with enough heat to melt you!

Jackson & Shay's story is epic - swoon-worthy & intensely emotional. Jackson just happens to be Shay's brother's best friend. He's also *seriously* easy on the eyes. Shay has a past, the kind of past she would most definitely like to forget. Past or not, Jackson is about to rock her world. Don't miss their story! Free on all retailers!

Burn For Me is a second chance romance for the ages. Sexy firefighters? Check. Rugged men? Check. Wrapped up together? Check. Brave the fire in this hot, small-town romance. Amelia & Cade were high school sweethearts & then it all fell apart. When they cross paths again, it's epic - don't miss Cade's story! Free on all retailers!

For more small town romance, take a visit to Last Frontier Lodge in Diamond Creek. A sexy, alpha SEAL meets his match with a brainy heroine in Take Me Home. Marley is all brains & Gage is all brawn. Sparks fly when their worlds collide. Don't miss Gage & Marley's story!
Free on all retailers!

If sports romance lights your spark, check out The Play. Liam is a British footballer who falls for Olivia, his doctor. A twist of forbidden heats up this swoon-worthy & laugh-out-loud romance. Don't miss Liam & Olivia's story.
Free on all retailers!

FIND MY BOOKS

Thank you for reading All It Takes! I hope you enjoyed the story. If so, you can help other readers find my books in a variety of ways.

1) Write a review!
2) Sign up for my newsletter, so you can receive information about upcoming new releases & receive a FREE copy of one of my books: http://jhcroixauthor.com/subscribe/
3) Like and follow my Amazon Author page at https://amazon.com/author/jhcroix
4) Follow me on Bookbub at https://www.bookbub.com/authors/j-h-croix
5) Follow me on Instagram at https://www.instagram.com/jhcroix/
6) Like my Facebook page at https://www.facebook.com/jhcroix

Visit my store to purchase ebooks & fun swag!
J.H. Croix Shop
Light My Fire Series
Wild With You
Hold Me Now
Only Ever Us
Fall For Me
Keep Me Close
With Every Breath
All It Takes
Take Me Now - coming August 2023!
Dare With Me Series
Crash Into You
Evers & Afters
Come To Me
Back To Us
Take Me There
After We Fall
Swoon Series
This Crazy Love
Wait For Me
Break My Fall
Truly Madly Mine
Still Go Crazy
If We Dare
Steal My Heart
Into The Fire Series
Burn For Me
Slow Burn
Burn So Bad
Hot Mess
Burn So Good
Sweet Fire
Play With Fire
Melt With You

Burn For You
Crash & Burn
That Snowy Night
Brit Boys Sports Romance
The Play
Big Win
Out Of Bounds
Play Me
Naughty Wish
Diamond Creek Alaska Novels
When Love Comes
Follow Love
Love Unbroken
Love Untamed
Tumble Into Love
Christmas Nights
Last Frontier Lodge Novels
Take Me Home
Love at Last
Just This Once
Falling Fast
Stay With Me
When We Fall
Hold Me Close
Crazy For You
Just Us

ACKNOWLEDGMENTS

To everyone who has supported my writing career (the list is loooooong), thank you, thank you, thank you. Extra thanks to my readers for reading my stories. Whether you found my books many moons ago, or this happens to be the first you've read, every chance you take on my stories keeps me writing.

Much gratitude to my editor and to Terri D. for helping me polish Wes & Tiffany's story and keep my days of the week straight. To my early readers for finding the stubborn errors and letting me know about them.

Najla Qamber continues to create gorgeous covers for this series and is so gracious with me. Big hugs to the bloggers, bookstagrammers, and booktokers who shout out their love of romance stories and spread the word to the world of readers.

My assistant helps keep me sane and sweeps up the details behind the scenes, and I'm forever grateful.

To my dogs who keep me company when I'm plotting and writing, and to my family for supporting me and my dreams.

xoxo
J.H. Croix